Romance Unbound Publishing

Presents

Heart of Submission

Claire Thompson

Edited by Jae Ashley

Cover Design by Kelly Shorten

ISBN 1452817731
EAN-13 9781452817736

Chapter 1

Kate Alexander sat at her computer, scrolling through images of women bound in rope and chain, their faces twisted in ecstasy. Even now she could almost feel the cold links of chain against heated flesh, the stinging curl of leather, the shiver of desire. She couldn't deny the tremble, the thrill of excitement these erotic images provoked in her. And why should she deny it?

Kate blew out a breath and reminded herself to focus. She had a deadline to get this novel written, but somehow the words just weren't flowing. She didn't know enough on her own to bring the story to life. She needed to get at the heart of the BDSM experience, pronto.

When her publisher had come to her, offering a contract for a BDSM novel and a sizable advance to go with it, she'd jumped at the chance. Her editor wanted something contemporary, maybe a mystery that takes place amidst the dark glitter of the BDSM underground leather scene. Or maybe a tale about another world—a fantasy world where all the humans are slaves, raised solely for the pleasure of the super-dominant species they are groomed to serve.

At first confident she could pull it off, so far Kate had started and stopped half a dozen times, thinking she was finally in the groove with a storyline, only to find herself slamming headlong into a creative brick wall. Promising plot lines fizzled into dead ends. She lacked the basis, the foundation and motivation for the stories. The characters were cartoons — two-dimensional paper cutouts instead of flesh and bone.

Why was she having such a hard time with this latest manuscript?

As if she didn't know.

Kate stood and stretched. Was it still there, she wondered? She moved toward the closet. Reaching for the top shelf, she felt along it for the small canvas bag she hadn't touched in nearly two years.

Retrieving it, she returned to her desk and sat down, plucking at the drawstring that held it closed. She pulled the coil of black leather from the bag, a single tail lash that was all that remained of their collection of BDSM gear.

She ran her fingers over the braided leather, recalling how Victor had recoiled in horror when she'd shyly asked him to use it on her. He'd been happy enough to go along with the playful spankings and light bondage, which at first had served to jumpstart a flagging relationship. She'd dared, bit by bit, to open up to him and admit her closely held secrets.

He had encouraged her, promising her she could tell him anything. She'd believed him; she'd trusted him.

She tried to explain her submissive and masochistic yearnings, daring for the first time to admit these feelings to another person. He claimed at first to understand, or at least to accept this part of her. But in the end he rejected the whole thing outright, telling her he "hadn't the stomach for her sick games any longer."

He had taken her trust—the sharing of her most secret and intimate desires, and had violated it, leaving her humiliated and ashamed in the process. Without meaning to, Kate allowed the experience to color her desire to explore the exotic and forbidden pleasures of sadomasochism, bondage and erotic discipline.

After Victor, she'd let go of what she'd told herself were immature longings to relinquish control at the hands of a strong man. She deliberately sought out vanilla guys, and never mentioned her secret fantasies of being held down and taken, of feeling the thrill of being bound and at the mercy of a dominant man who took what he wanted.

In the two years since Victor had left her, she'd dated, but not seriously. After all with a busy life and successful career, who had time? Writing under the pen name of Ashley Kendall, Kate had fourteen erotic romance novels to her credit. When she was focused, she could write an entire novel in two months, working from before dawn till late in the night. When she was in the groove, nothing in this world was so satisfying or all–encompassing.

She had thought she could bring the story to life by drawing on the experience she'd had with Victor, and while she could recall the sting of a whip and the grip of rope, something was blocking her from accessing the emotions that went along with it.

Maybe the Internet would get her creative juices flowing. She did a search on BDSM. She started at the various blogs and websites that claimed some authority on the subject, dutifully making notes and jotting down possible story ideas.

BDSM 101, that's what she needed. Why didn't she think of that sooner? She lived only an hour outside of Manhattan. Something was always going on there, surely. Kate did another search on BDSM events in the area and a whole host of options popped up.

She checked out a dozen potentially promising venues, only to find they were happening across the country, or had already just happened the weekend before, or weren't scheduled until six months from now. Well, what had she expected? A readymade program, tailored just for aspiring BDSM authors who were also considering a personal reentry into the scene?

She was just about to give up when something caught her eye. Before wasting any time, she checked the location. New York City. And the date—this coming weekend!

BDSM Immersion Weekend. A three-day intensive program hosted by Power Play. Workshops including the Master/slave Dynamic, Discipline and Correction, Flogging *and Whipping from the Basics to the Sublime, The Art of Pain – Giving and Receiving, Sensual Bondage Techniques, and more! Play parties at night. Couples and singles welcome. Space is limited. Email Jacob Presley (<u>MasterPresley@gmail.com</u>) for pricing and other details.*

What a perfect way to ease back into the scene with no strings attached. She could drink it all in, attending the seminars and workshops to get back into the swing of things, while taking mental notes for her novel.

The play parties she wasn't so sure about. She'd never been to a BDSM play party, though Victor and she had toyed with the idea. She was aware they were sometimes little more than orgies, with a few whips and chains thrown in for effect.

Though she doubted this particular venue would be like that, a single woman without a partner was still probably prey for all the losers and posers who couldn't get a woman on their own. *If* she attended the evening parties, she'd keep her wits sharp and her clothes on.

"Are you really going to do this?" she said aloud.

"Why not?" she answered herself, ignoring the flutter of nerves in her belly. She was an independent woman ready for a weekend adventure. There was nothing and no one holding her back.

Opening her email account, she typed in Master Presley's address, dashed off an inquiry and hit send before she could change her mind.

~*~

Master Presley was a tall man, easily over six feet four inches. He must have weighed over three hundred pounds but he carried it well, his girth imposing. Though plain, his face was kind, his smile crooked but genuine.

Master Presley signed Kate in and gave her a pamphlet outlining the various workshops and seminars that were to take place over the course of the weekend. There were already a few dozen folks milling in the large, open space of the warehouse. There were no windows, but the place was filled with light from skylights overhead. A buffet breakfast was laid out on two long tables, flanked at either end by coffee urns.

Some people were sitting at the picnic tables set up for the purpose, but most were standing, plates and cups balanced, chatting in clusters. They all seemed like they knew each other. Probably many of them did. Kate had had to fork over the annual membership fee to Power Play in addition to the cost of the event, but told herself it was worth it—all in the name of research for her novel, and thus tax deductible.

"Help yourself to coffee and some breakfast," Master Presley said, patting her arm. "The first seminar starts at noon. You can leave your bag in the lockers until you're ready to check in at the motel." He pointed toward a row of tall metal lockers that ran along a portion of one wall of the warehouse. Beside the lockers was a rack that contained dozens of whips, floggers, crops and canes. Kate stared at them, her heart doing a little flip flop.

The man followed her gaze. "Nice, huh? Most of that belongs to Marianne and Marty. They're the cofounders of the group and run a serious BDSM Dungeon in Westchester County, very posh, very upscale."

He returned his gaze to Kate, appraising her with a tilted head. "I hear they're looking for sub girls for hire. You could make a pretty penny in tips, a lovely girl like you. No sex, you just let the guys tie you up and such. Extra for rough play. Don't worry, they're very careful. No permanent marks or cutting. Should I tell them you're interested?"

Kate realized her mouth had fallen open. She snapped it shut. "No, that's okay. I'm—I'm kind of new to all this. Going to take my time."

Master Presley looked disappointed, but he nodded. "Probably wise." He looked down at a clipboard and then back up at her. "Your roommate is Stacey. That's her over there. The short one with the beehive hairdo." He pointed toward a round little woman somewhere in her late thirties, with light brown hair piled into a teased, sprayed dome on her head and eyes ringed in black eyeliner that brought Cleopatra to mind. She was squeezed into a black leather dress a few sizes too small, her deep cleavage accentuated by the tight bodice. Short, pudgy legs were encased in knee-high black leather boots with stiletto heels. Though Kate found the ensemble over the top, somehow the woman managed to pull it off.

She looked back at Master Presley as he handed her a preprinted nametag. It read *Ashley* against a white background. It had seemed wiser to use her pen name for this venture—who knew what oddballs might track her down otherwise. She noticed the tray had other tags remaining, some white, some red. "What's the color significance?" she asked.

"Red is for Top, Dom or Master, white for bottom, sub or slave, depending on what folks are into." She noticed his tag was red. She'd filled out a questionnaire as part of the admission process to the weekend, answering personal questions about her interests and orientation in the scene. She wasn't entirely sure how she felt about being pre-designated as a sub, but she shrugged. This was for her novel. It wasn't as if she was really going to be an ongoing member in this BDSM group.

A couple came in behind her to sign in and Kate moved toward the lockers. Finding an empty one, she stashed her duffel bag inside and wandered toward the breakfast table. She headed toward the coffee urn, hoping they had real cream or at least half and half.

That's when she saw him.

The man, with a thick swatch of blond hair falling over his forehead, was dressed in black. Black silk encased broad shoulders, narrowing down his body toward black jeans that molded against long muscular legs. He was wearing black boots, the toes square, the leather scuffed. He looked to be in his early thirties, and his tag was red, though she couldn't see the name on it from where she stood.

"Where have you been all my life?"

Startled, Kate turned toward the voice. A man about her height of five-foot-eight with a tangle of dark curls hanging nearly to his shoulders was smiling at her. He, too, was dressed in black, wearing a tank top that showed off a slender but well-muscled frame, over black jeans. Though he wasn't bad looking, Kate was still fixated on the image of the blond god.

"Oh, hi," she said, forcing herself to pay attention.

"Your first Power Play weekend?" he asked, moving closer.

She stepped back. "Yes."

"Here alone?"

"Um..."

The man laughed. "Relax. I'm not going to eat you. You'll find this is a very respectful group. We pride ourselves on offering a safe, sane and consensual environment for the exploration of all things BDSM." The man's tag was red, the name *Sir James* printed on it. "Not to mention, my wife would kill me if she thought I was hitting on you."

He laughed again, offering a small wave toward a tall, imposing woman who stood near the buffet, piling her plate with scrambled eggs and bacon. She wore a long dress of flowing black silk, a thick black leather collar around her neck.

Trying not to be too obvious about it, Kate scanned the small crowd for the handsome blond, but he was nowhere in sight. With an inward sigh, she got herself some coffee. Sir James had followed her, talking steadily. His partner approached them, introductions were made and Kate listened as they talked about which seminars and workshops would be fun to attend.

Stacey joined them a moment later. "Ah, the newbie. I hear you're to be my roomie." She swept Kate from head to toe with a brazen gaze. "Welcome my friend, to the fun that never ends. You're gonna knock 'em dead. I'll be happy to take your cast-offs." She laughed, the sound oddly high-pitched compared to her smoky speaking voice.

"Oh, I'm just here to learn," Kate said, embarrassed.

"Yeah, right," Stacey rejoined with a snort. "Me too." She winked conspiratorially.

Hoping to deflect this line of talk, Kate offered, "So, you're an active player in the scene?" Might as well start her research now.

"Not as active as I'd like, honey," Stacey quipped. "Now, if I had a bod like yours, and all that glorious hair…" She reached out, fingering Kate's hair. "All you need is a little hairspray and I could fix you right up." Eyeing Stacey's elaborate fifties hairdo, Kate made a mental note to reject *that* offer.

Stacey waved suddenly toward someone across the room. "Be right back. Gotta say hi to an old pal." As Stacey walked away, Kate stepped back, bumping against someone behind her. The automatic apology died on her lips as she turned, her coffee sloshing over the rim of the cup.

He had eyes the color of clear dark tea, sunny blond hair spilling carelessly over a high forehead, a half smile hovering on full, sensuous lips. His red tag read *Master John*, though she didn't need color coding or titles to ascertain his orientation. He exuded power. Kate could feel it like fingers moving over her skin. She realized she was staring at him. Swallowing, she turned away, hoping the heat in her face hadn't translated to a blush.

She felt his hand on her shoulder, gently but forcibly turning her back toward him. "Ashley," he said, reading her tag. Looking back at her face, his smile was warm enough to melt butter. "I bet you're a wild one, in serious need of taming."

Kate realized her nipples had shot to attention without permission. Silently she cursed the flimsy fabric of her cream-colored silk tank top. As if reading her mind, Master John's eyes moved slowly downward from her face, sweeping over her breasts.

She tossed her hair. "I might be wild, but I've yet to meet the man who can tame me," she said with as much bravado as she could muster.

Shit! Where had that come from?

Master John laughed. "Is that a challenge, little girl?"

Returning to her senses, Kate stammered, "Uh, no. No, I'm just here to learn. To take it all in."

"Are you now," he replied, eyebrows arched.

"Yep." Kate was disconcerted by the knowing smile in his deep brown eyes.

"Well, I do hope you'll attend my seminar on whipping technique. Perhaps I can talk you into being my volunteer."

"No thanks, I'll pass," Kate said, ignoring her thumping heart.

Master John said nothing, but he stared deep into her eyes with an expression so intense she couldn't look away, even if she'd wanted to. For that moment it was as if the whole room went silent and still, though surely that was Kate's imagination. She found herself tumbling into the man's powerful gaze. Her mouth had gone dry, her pussy the opposite.

Suddenly the room switched back on, as Stacey appeared beside them. "Ah, you've met Master John," she said. "Figures, the beautiful people naturally gravitate toward one another."

While Kate struggled to recover herself, Master John turned to the small woman. "I was just asking Ashley here to volunteer as my whipping girl, but she refused. You interested?"

"You know it, babe." Stacey laughed. "You can do things with a bullwhip that make a masochist swoon." She winked at Kate, offering in a stage whisper, "I bet his bullwhip isn't the only thing that could make a girl swoon."

Someone was calling Master John, and he swiveled toward the voice. "Later, lovely ladies." As they watched him move away, Stacey sighed and shook her head. "Figures. The newbie wins the prize. Not that I'm surprised. He always chooses the best looking girl to set his sights on."

"What?" Kate suddenly felt like she was in high school again, the focus of the captain of the football team. She'd hated high school, and didn't welcome the feeling.

"Master John. If he chooses you to play with tonight, you'll be sure to get your money's worth."

"Oh, I'm not here to — "

"Spare me, honey. We're all here for one thing. Might as well admit it and have some fun."

Kate stared at Stacey, trying to form a retort, but no words came. Maybe Stacey was right. Maybe Kate should just kick back and enjoy it. What the hell? It was her secret adventure. She could reinvent herself, just for this one weekend. After all, it was Ashley Kendall who was attending. Kate Alexander could remain safely hidden, watching from the sidelines, taking notes.

Chapter 2

Kate settled down cross-legged next to Stacey on a large throw pillow in a corner of the warehouse. After mingling for a while longer that morning, they'd gone together to check in to the motel, a functional space with barely room enough for two beds and a bureau of some kind of yellowish brown material that yearned to be wood. The room had poorly plastered walls and a bathroom the size of a small closet. Stacey shrugged off the meager accommodations, assuring Kate with a broad wink that she wouldn't be spending much time in it anyway, so who cared.

They'd sat through a required speech by Marianne and Marty, or M&M as they liked to call themselves, the partners who had started Power Play a few years back. They'd talked from a stage that had been set up in another corner, outlining the rules and regulations for the event to the group of people sitting on folding chairs. Kate had looked for but hadn't seen Master John. Maybe he was exempt from the rules, or already knew them by heart.

As far as she could tell, pretty much anything went. Since it wasn't a public venue, the rules that applied to BDSM clubs, such as "no exchange of bodily fluids" didn't apply here. Sex and nudity were fine, as long as everyone involved was having fun. They harped on the usual bywords of safe, sane and consensual, and briefly outlined the rules, including negotiating the limits of a scene in advance and using Power Play's standard safeword of "red". They reviewed proper etiquette when it came to watching other people's scenes, which included staying quiet, showing respect and never interrupting unless someone appeared to be in danger.

Everything was optional — you could attend what you wanted in the way of seminars and workshops, or just spend your entire time in the dungeon devising scenes of your own. The dungeon had been set up in the basement of the warehouse, and Stacey assured Kate she wouldn't want to miss it.

But for now they were waiting for the Sensual Bondage Techniques class to start. There were eight couples situated around a small dais, if Kate and Stacey could be called a couple. Many of them had various lengths of rope and other implements set out in front of them. Stacey told Kate it didn't matter if they didn't have their own stuff. Chase would provide it.

"Chase is a bondage expert. I've been to this class before. It's fun. He's very hands-on." Stacey waggled her eyebrows and hugged herself suggestively, making Kate laugh.

The man in question chose that moment to step onto the small dais in front of them. He was carrying a large duffel bag, which he set down beside him. He was about five foot ten inches, with wavy dark brown hair in a kind of shaggy cut, the bangs too long over his eyes, hair curling down the back of his neck. He had very blue eyes — an unusually dark blue, and three days stubble on a pleasant if unremarkable face. Unlike most of the folks decked out in their Goth and SM gear, he was wearing a white button down shirt tucked into faded jeans with a prominent hole in the left knee. On his feet were sneakers of no discernable brand.

He was the opposite of Master John, Kate thought. Instead of giving her the jitters, he was easygoing, calming somehow. Instead of exciting her, he relaxed her.

"Greetings." He smiled toward the group. There was a smattering of applause and a few greetings called out in return. "My name is Chase Saunders. Most of you know me but I do see a few new faces." He looked at Kate, and the smile he offered her transformed his face from ordinary to lively and warm. Despite herself, Kate found herself smiling back. She relaxed for the first time that day, easing into the cushions.

His eyes still on Kate, Chase continued. "There's a whole gamut of bondage techniques and we could spend literally a solid week and still not cover it all. Rope can be used in a utilitarian manner for the simple binding of a bottom for play or display, or it can be used as an art form, as in the case of classic Japanese Shibari rope bondage.

"For this particular seminar we won't be getting into the really complex knots that can drive a bottom nuts." There was scattered laughter. "You know what I'm talking about." Chase grinned, looking over the group. "Your partner wants to be tied up, but they just don't appreciate your beautiful knot work that's taking way the fuck too long. I'll show you three ties that can be done in under five minutes, but will still give your partner what they seek." He fixed his eyes on Kate. "The tight, inescapable feel of rope against skin."

Kate swallowed, her wrists suddenly tingling at the lack of rope. She rubbed them, aware of a prick of desire deep inside. Before Victor had categorically decided that what they were doing was sick, perverted and wrong, they had engaged in some bondage, though it had never been as intense or restrictive as Kate would have liked. Mostly just tying her spread eagle to the bed, and some light breast bondage.

Chase, his attention now on the couple beside Kate and Stacey, continued. "Whether they're into comfortable long-term bondage or more restrictive short-term binds, these ties will work." He picked up a length of soft white rope, twisting it in his hands.

"The way that you handle the ropes can create a romantic scene. When most folks think of having sex with their partner tied up, they think of the spread eagle bed tie. Which is fine as far as it goes, but there's so much more you can do. We'll learn basic parallel limb ties, wrist-to-ankle, frog-ties and lots more.

"For you total newbies, I'll show you basic knots and positions and we'll talk about technique, safety considerations and the type of rope everyone should have in their play kit." He jumped down from the dais. "Okay. Let's get started. I need a victim, er, volunteer." Laughter. "Anyone?"

He approached Stacey and Kate, who were sitting closest to the dais. Reading her nametag, he said, "Ashley. I haven't seen you here before. New to the scene?"

Before Kate could reply, Stacey piped up. "She's just moved here from Paris. Doesn't speak a word of English. Pick me, Chase. I'll be your volunteer. Let's work on those sex positions." Stacey popped up, smoothing her leather skirt over her thighs.

The group laughed, Chase included. "Paris, huh?" he said, eyeing Kate once more.

"Lower Hudson Valley," Kate admitted, before recalling she was incognito. "Stacey's got an active imagination."

Chase smiled. "That she does." He turned toward Stacey, his smile perhaps a bit rueful. "I guess I have my volunteer then." He led her up to the dais and demonstrated a few simple positions. Kate silently marveled at how at ease Stacey seemed to be with herself. It had the effect of making her far more attractive than when Kate had first laid eyes on her — had it only been a few hours before? Something about being truly comfortable in your own skin was a definite turn-on. It was something, even at thirty-two, Kate knew she had yet to master.

Stacey returned to the mat beside Kate as Chase moved from couple to couple, working hands-on while keeping up a running commentary. Stacey and Kate took turns practicing the knots and bondage positions on each other, and Kate found herself really enjoying the workshop. Chase was informative, funny and easy to listen to.

Though they were only fooling around, Kate couldn't deny the sexual thrill that edged through her when Stacey bound her in various positions, or the delicious feeling of erotic helplessness being bound engendered in her. Without invitation, Master John slipped into her mind. What if, instead of Stacey, he was beside her now, raking her body with that burning stare? Or murmuring something sexy in her ear while he secured her wrists and upper arms behind her back with a few simple but effective knots? Would Kate kneel up, legs spread wide, and permit him to bind her wrists to her thighs, leaving her open to him as his fingers slid between her legs, seeking her sweet spot, claiming her…

Kate shook her head, embarrassed at her musings, glad no one else could see into her head. What was she *thinking*? Well, that was just it. She wasn't thinking. She was letting her body do the thinking for her. She pressed her legs together, willing the ache in her pussy to subside.

Later that afternoon, Kate found herself in the front row beside Stacey for Master John's seminar on whipping techniques. This one was held on the stage and was more widely attended than the bondage workshop had been. Though it was five minutes past the start time, Master John was nowhere in sight.

There was someone on the stage however. A young slender Asian woman with long dark hair was kneeling there, her eyes down, her hands resting on her thighs, palms upward. Around her neck was a red leather collar, with matching cuffs secured around delicate wrists. She was dressed in a thong and a black waist cincher, her small, high breasts bare above it. The contrast of red rosebud lips, pale skin and the black of the cincher and her silky hair was striking.

Kate was usually comfortable with her height, once she'd outgrown the praying mantis gawkiness of her teenage years, but looking at the graceful petite figure before her, she suddenly felt large and gangly by comparison.

"She's beautiful," Kate murmured.

"She needs a sandwich," Stacey retorted.

"Does she, uh, belong to Master John?" Kate asked, telling herself it didn't matter one way or the other.

"No. She's George's latest toy." Stacey gestured toward a slight, balding man with a receding chin and prominent ears, flanked by two women, both of whom wore the same red collars and wrists cuffs worn by the woman on stage. "He collects slaves. Always brings at least three with him to these things. I don't know what he's got—it sure ain't looks. Probably money, and lots of it. I've met Jen and Gretchen, the two next to him, but the Asian girl toy is new. Calls herself Lotus Flower." Stacey snorted.

Just then the audience broke into polite applause. Master John came onto the stage and turned toward the group, flashing a perfect, white smile right at Kate. "Ash, he's staring straight at you," Stacey whispered, nudging Kate sharply in the ribs. It took Kate a fraction of a second to process the use of Ash, before remembering she'd signed up with her pen name.

"He is not," she denied reflexively, though he did seem to be. Ridiculously, she felt herself coloring. She hadn't blushed this much since high school, and it was annoying the crap out of her. So what if he was handsome and dominant? She was here for research, not to pick up a guy, no matter how GQ perfect he might be.

Master John stepped toward a low table at the back of the stage that Kate hadn't noticed before, distracted as she'd been by the petite beauty. There were several whips and floggers laid out on the table. Master John selected an ominous looking plaited single tail whip, letting it unfurl as he moved toward center stage.

He paused beside the girl, stroking back the curtain of shiny black hair as he bent to murmur something to her. Apparently satisfied with her response, he returned to the front of the stage and addressed the audience. "I was going to start with flogging and move you slowly along the continuum." He spoke with a slight Southern accent she hadn't noticed when they'd been speaking one-on-one. It had a pleasing lilt, maybe Georgian, she thought. She could just picture him with a cowboy hat perched on his head, mounted astride a stallion, posing shirtless for one of those eye candy calendars. She tried to focus on what he was saying. "But I figured you all have been there, done that. Lotus Flower has graciously agreed, so we'll be moving directly to a bullwhip demo instead."

He gestured toward George. "If that's okay with you, George."

George nodded. "Excellent," John said, his eyes narrowing. He moved toward the edge of the stage and held up the long, imposing whip. "This, my friends, was handmade by Adam Simon." There were murmurs of approval.

"Adam's a master whip maker out of Australia," Stacey explained. "His stuff is ridiculously expensive. Uses the leather from a rare breed of yak found only in Tibet."

Kate wrinkled her nose. "You're kidding right?"

"Uh...yeah." Stacey laughed, shaking her head. "Actually I think it's kangaroo hide. Weird enough though, huh."

Kate nodded.

Master John held up the whip. "If you're thinking about buying one of these babies, this is one of the best there is. It's made from kangaroo hide, which is the strongest type of leather for its weight in the world."

Stacey turned toward Kate with a triumphant grin. "Do I know my bullwhips or what?" Kate smiled back. She hadn't planned on liking Stacey, but found herself doing so anyway.

Master John's voice had taken on a different tone, what Kate would have called lecture mode, if he'd been a professor. "Kangaroo hide is the best for fine plaited work of eight strands or more, which this one is." He ran his hand along the plaited leather. "But I wouldn't recommend eight strands as a starter. It can be hard to handle. If you're just getting into bullwhips, I would suggest a four plait stock whip or bullwhip, since they're hard wearing and aren't the price of a small car like this baby."

There was laughter, and someone called out. "Enough talking—let's see it in action."

All at once Master John flicked the whip out toward the audience, the sharp crack causing Kate and several others to gasp and flinch. Master John offered a lazy smile. "Patience, Frank," he said to the man who'd called out, "is a virtue not only subs need to cultivate, apparently."

The group laughed. Kate noticed the girl on stage still hadn't moved. How in the world did she kneel there like that? Kate would have been fidgeting all over the place by now, no question. Still ignoring the girl, Master John continued. "As I just demonstrated, a bullwhip's length, flexibility, and tapered design allow it to be thrown in such a way that, towards the end of the throw, part of the whip exceeds the speed of sound, thereby creating a small sonic boom. It's all in the wrist. The force required from the person holding the whip is very minimal to make it crack. It only requires a change of direction or a change in speed."

As he continued the lecture, Kate found she too would rather see a demonstration than listen to him go on and on. Chase had talked a lot of shop too, she recalled, but he'd done so while demonstrating, or helping someone in the group in a very hands-on approach. Of course, she told herself, Master John couldn't very well do that with a bullwhip. Still, as he droned on she found herself suppressing a yawn.

"A bullwhip consists of a handle section, a thong, a fall, and a cracker. The main portion is the thong, this braided part here." She zoned out for a few minutes, thinking about a possible plotline, but her attention was sharply recalled by a second sonic cracking of the whip.

"Stand up, Lotus Flower. It's time to give them what they came for." Master John's voice lowered into a seductive purr, the lecturing tone gone. Gracefully the young woman rose to her feet, which were bare. "Turn around, bend over and grab your ankles. Don't come out of position until I tell you."

Lotus Flower nodded, her face serene. Kate marveled at how calm she was, half-naked on a stage, waiting to feel the sharp sting of that dangerous looking whip. No way in hell would Kate ever volunteer for *that*!

The girl assumed the ordered position, her legs perfectly straight. Peering more closely, Kate detected marks along Lotus Flower's small, round ass and slender thighs, pale lines that had faded with time, crisscrossed with fresher, darker welts still healing.

"Is that okay, do you think?" Kate whispered to Stacey. "She's already marked."

Stacey shrugged. "George's girls always take a lot. Don't worry, Master John knows what he's doing. He wouldn't have accepted her as a volunteer if it wasn't safe."

Kate nodded, though she wasn't convinced. Not that she knew anything — a few months of experimentation a few years back did not her an expert make. Trying to suspend her anxiety, she focused on the stage, her gut clenching in nervous anticipation.

Master John stood to the side of the bent girl and flicked the wrist of his whip hand. The sharp crack split the air and again Kate flinched. The girl flinched too — her first reaction. A long white line appeared on her left ass cheek that quickly changed to red. A second later Master John added an identical stripe to the other side. The girl cried out but remained in position.

Master John turned to the audience. "I've been doing this for ten years. This is not something you pick up overnight. If you want to learn, see me after and I'll give you my card. I offer group and individual sessions."

He turned back toward the girl, drawing his hand over her ass, his fingers tracing the fresh welts he'd created there. Kate swallowed, watching him, her body tingling as if his hand was on her, not the girl. The room was silent. Master John stepped back and snapped the whip several times in rapid succession. When the cracker curled cruelly against Lotus Flower's bare thigh, she screamed and stumbled forward.

"Back in position, girl. Now." Master John's voice was suddenly hard. Kate found herself feeling terribly sorry for Lotus Flower. She imagined herself up there, and knew she wouldn't get back in position. She'd probably grab the whip from Master John and give him a bit of his own medicine. So much for being submissive, she thought to herself with a wry inward grin.

But Lotus Flower dutifully bent over again, grabbing narrow ankles with slender hands. Master John stroked her back. "That's right," he said. "You can take a little more for me. I know you can."

He turned back to the audience. Kate's eyes traveled over his physique. No question, the man was *very* easy on the eyes. "The crack of a bullwhip explodes like a thunderbolt. It's both savage and sensuous, dangerous and sexy as hell," he pronounced.

Like you, Kate found herself thinking. The girl stood still as stone, her welted ass toward the audience. Master John turned back to her. "Four more," he pronounced. "Show us your grace." Four more cracks, two on each cheek, each punctuated by a soft cry from the girl, though she managed this time to hold her position.

Master John coiled the whip and set it down on the table. He tapped Lotus Flower's shoulder and she rose, turning slowly to face the audience, her cheeks flushed. Master John stroked the hair from her face and put his arm lightly around her bare shoulders.

"Thank you, Lotus Flower. I'm sure your Master will want to work with you on maintaining position."

"Yes, Sir," the girl said in a clear, high voice. She dropped to her knees and bent low, kissing the top of Master John's right boot. The audience applauded.

As Master John helped Lotus Flower down the three steps leading to the stage, Stacey turned to Kate. "So, what'd you think? You ready to play tonight? You know he's going to ask you."

"I know no such thing," Kate asserted, though the idea excited her as much as it unnerved her. "I'm not even sure I'm going to the play party."

"Not going to the party!" Stacey shouted, her voice ripe with incredulity. Several people sitting nearby turned to stare at them. Lowering her volume only slightly, Stacey added, "Come on now, Ashley. You have to go. I won't let you *not* go. The parties are the reason we're here, babe. All this seminar and workshop shit—it's just foreplay. You have to *promise* me you're going. Otherwise I'll sell you into slavery to Georgie Boy. You think I'm kidding, but I got connections."

Stacey furrowed her brows and frowned, though her small dark eyes were dancing.

In spite of herself, Kate laughed. "Okay, okay, I'll go. But no one's getting near me with a bullwhip, I can tell you that right now. Give me a flogger any day. It's more, I don't know, sensual. Less punitive."

"Punitive," Stacey repeated. "I like that. You have a way with words, you know that? You should be a writer."

Kate smiled. "You think so?"

Chapter 3

"**T**ighter."

"You sure you'll be able to breathe?" Kate stood just behind Stacey, who was bent over the bed with Kate's foot on her butt. Kate was pulling at the thick black satin ties of Stacey's custom-made corset. "It's like something out of *Gone with the Wind*," she offered, as Stacey's round form began to assume a more hourglass shape.

"Except Scarlet's waist was the size of one of my thighs." Stacey laughed.

Finally satisfied with Kate's efforts, Stacey stood and turned, offering Kate a view of ample breasts bared nearly to the nipple. The red satin corset fit over a tight black leather miniskirt, the tops of her fishnet thigh highs visible beneath its hem. Stacey moved toward the mirror on the back of the bathroom door. Putting her hands on her hips, she announced, "I look fabulous."

"You sure do. You look great! Maybe I should get one of those."

"It set me back a small fortune, but it's worth it. Which brings us to the question. What are you going to wear tonight? Let's see what you brought."

"Well, you know I hadn't really planned on the party thing..." Kate spread her meager offerings on the bed. She had a pair of black linen pants and a pale green silk sleeveless blouse, plus a sleeveless black dress that zipped up the back.

"This is it? This is what you bring to a BDSM play weekend?" Stacey's tone was disbelieving. "You're kidding right? Where's the bustier? The stockings? Your stilettos?"

"I'm tall enough, thanks," Kate demurred. "And I don't have enough to put in a bustier."

"Sure you do, honey." Stacey eyed Kate's chest. Kate was still wearing the clothes she'd arrived in that morning. "I know," Stacey said, her smile suddenly cunning. "You don't have the gear, but you *definitely* have the bod. And you're right—sometimes understatement is the way to go." She ran her hands down her crimson corset and laughed. "Not for me, of course. I'm an in-your-face kind of gal. But for you..." Stacey squinted, sizing Kate up.

She turned toward the bed and picked up the silk blouse. "This will be perfect, *without* the bra."

Kate instinctively covered her chest. "Oh, no. I couldn't..."

"Of *course* you could! You have gorgeous tits. The kind that stand up on their own, all perky like round peaches on a plate. You got it, flaunt it!" Stacey shook her head. "Man, I'd kill for a body like that. You should be proud of what you got, babe."

Kate said nothing, but her mind was whirring. Stacey was right. At the risk of being immodest, Kate did have a good body and she knew it. Unlike most women she knew, she didn't feel like she needed to lose a few pounds. She ran several times a week and lifted weights as a way to unwind while watching TV. And it wasn't like she was attending a book signing. This was a BDSM sex play party, for god's sake. Yeah, she was there to do research for her novel, but who said she couldn't have fun in the process?

As if reading her mind, Stacey nodded. "So, that's settled. Hurry up and shower and dress, and I'll do your makeup." Kate looked at Stacey, with her heavy eyeliner, dark blue sparkling eyelids and a red gash of a mouth.

"No, that's okay. I can do my own—"

Stacey laughed. "Re*lax*. I know you can't pull off the slave slut girl look. But we can add some color at least. A little pizzazz. Trust me. I went to cosmetology school."

~*~

The dungeon filled the entire basement of the warehouse. Large rugs had been strewn over the cement floors and sconces shaped like old-fashioned torches lined the walls, which had been painted red. Some kind of new age jazz was being piped in through small speakers mounted in the ceiling corners of the room.

The space had been partitioned into at least a dozen private and semi-private areas by large folding screens. Thick concrete support posts spaced at strategic intervals had been converted to whipping posts, with manacles and cuffs hanging from wooden mounts that could be adjusted for height.

There were three St. Andrew's crosses, a bondage wheel, several cages, a number of medical exam tables complete with leather straps, and piles of pillows heaped here and there. Along one wall was a large aluminum frame strung with a thick weave of rubber strips in a spider web design.

The cache of toys Kate had seen upstairs earlier in the day had been brought down to the dungeon and Master Presley stood beside it, helping people select the implement of their choice, and signing the item out on his clipboard.

The party appeared to be just getting started when Stacey and Kate arrived. There had been a number of people upstairs milling around, talking and eating snacks, and it seemed like even more down in the dungeon. Most of them were dressed more like Stacey than Kate, decked out in black leather, fetish rubber gear, or very little at all. Kate saw Lotus Flower and George's other two slaves dressed in identical black waist cinchers, each with a leash attached around their necks, being pulled along by George toward the spider web. A tall, very thin man was wearing nothing except a small cage locked around his cock and balls. He too was leashed, though the leash was tethered to his cock cage, and he was being led by another man, dressed predictably in black leather.

"I don't remember there being this many people here before," Kate commented, taking it all in.

"Some folks can't get here till after work," Stacey explained. "Speaking of which, what do you do to pay the bills?"

Kate was saved from answering by a tall, heavyset man who suddenly appeared before them and swung Stacey up into his arms. "Baby! Your lord and master is here at last. You ready to suffer for me, gorgeous?"

Stacey let out a delighted peel of laughter. "You know it, Tim, er, I mean Sir Tim."

The man set her down and offered a mock frown. "Uh oh, you know the rules. When in the dungeon, it's always Sir. Now I'll have to punish you." He pulled a tapered red candle from his back pocket and ran it under his nose, as if smelling a fine cigar.

Stacey turned to Kate. "Ashley, I want you to meet my dear friend, *Sir* Tim. We used to be lovers until we figured out we drove each other nuts, but we still enjoy playing at parties. No one can handle hot wax like this guy."

Tim bowed toward Kate. "The pleasure is mine." Turning to Stacey he said, "Where did you find this delectable young thing? Is she part of the two for one package I signed up for?" He stared hard at Kate's chest. She crossed her arms, embarrassed. How had she let Stacey talk her into going braless? The blouse was so sheer she might as well have been topless, her nipples clearly outlined against the pale, thin fabric.

"She might be. Depends on her. What do you say, Ash? Ever experience the fiery thrill of hot wax dripping over your delicate parts? There's nothing like it," Stacey said, hugging herself with apparent anticipation.

"Can't say as I have," Kate replied. "I've heard a few horror stories around hot wax. With my luck, my hair would catch on fire and the guy would end up calling the fire department."

Sir Tim grinned, shaking his head. "Safety is the name of the game, especially where fire is concerned." He puffed out his chest. "Luckily, you're with a pro tonight. We'll give you a demo. I've got everything all set up already." He turned to Stacey. "Let's give 'em a show, shall we?"

Stacey took the man's offered arm and they moved off toward a partitioned area, her high heels clacking on the concrete floor. Kate followed, aware of eyes on her as she moved, relieved no one was approaching her.

Sir Tim helped Stacey onto a medical exam table and slipped a small pillow beneath her head. He placed Velcro cuffs on Stacey's wrists and she let her hands drop to either side of the table. Crouching beside the table, Sir Tim secured her wrists beneath it with a length of chain attached there for the purpose. Next he pulled a thick leather strap across her chest, which he buckled securely just below her breasts.

Kate was standing off to the side of the table, wondering what to do with herself. Stacey turned toward her and smiled. "Relax, Ash. This is fun.

Hopefully you're next, eh?" Kate didn't reply, though she seriously doubted she would be next. Several people had come to stand beside her. A few of them greeted Sir Tim by name.

There was a card table set up against the screen, and on it were three tall jar candles with pictures of the Virgin Mary staring mournfully upward, plus a bottle of mineral oil, a bowl of ice, a washcloth and a box of matches.

Sir Tim selected one of the jar candles. Opening the box of kitchen matches, he pulled one out and struck it against the side of the box. A small flame flared. He lit the candle and returned both it and the matchbox to the table.

Leaning over Stacey, he put his hand between her legs, moving his fingers beneath the leather skirt. He smiled a sly smile. "Wet for me already, eh, slave girl?" For the first time, Stacey had no ready comeback. Kate noticed her cheeks were flushed, her eyes fever-bright. When they began to flutter shut, Tim removed his hand and focused on Stacey's breasts. He pulled at them, popping each one from the satin corset that had barely held them in place. Stacey's nipples looked like large, fat pink gum drops at the center of soft, creamy mounds of flesh. Tim leaned over, burying his face between them. "Oh, I've missed these," he said, longing and reverence in his voice.

"They've missed you, Sir," Stacey murmured.

Sir Tim picked up the bottle of mineral oil from the table and squirted some onto Stacey's breasts and thighs. He rubbed it in, coating her skin with the shiny oil. That done, he retrieved the burning candle. "Ready, slave girl?"

"Yes, please, Sir," Stacey responded in her smoky voice.

He tipped the candle and a trail of black wax splashed over Stacey's left breast. When the droplets coated her nipple, Stacey blew out a sudden breath, her eyes squeezed tight. Kate's nipples ached with sympathy. What would it feel like, she wondered? Did she have the nerve to climb up onto the table after Stacey?

"What do you say?" Sir Tim intoned.

"Thank you, Sir," Stacey hissed between clenched teeth.

"Good girl." He turned his attention to her second breast, eliciting a similar reaction from the bound woman. After covering most of her bared flesh with splashes of hot wax, Sir Tim moved downward, focusing on the pale skin showing above Stacey's stockings.

Stacey twitched, shuddered and moaned as melted wax splashed over her skin. Kate wanted to turn away, yet found herself riveted to the scene. She watched, along with the small crowd now gathered around the table, as Sir Tim lifted the hem of the leather skirt.

Kate held her breath as Sir Tim tilted the candle over the expanse of shaven, pale skin. Stacey's eyes were squeezed tight, her lips compressed in a tight line, her nostrils flaring. When the first drops splashed against her pubic mound, she yelped, then stilled. He did it again and again, until the black wax coating created a triangle where once pubic hair had been.

"Spread your legs. Offer yourself to me, slave girl." Sir Tim's voice was low, the jaunty, teasing tone with which they'd begun the scene replaced with something compelling and dominant. Despite herself, Kate reacted to the words as if they'd been spoken directly to her. She caught her breath and swallowed. Though she wasn't attracted to the man in the slightest, something about the masterful change in his demeanor spoke to her on a primal level.

Reality intervened when Stacey spread her ample thighs and arched her hips upward, flashing all who cared to look. Kate didn't want to see Stacey's spread pussy, and the thought of melted wax dripped over tender labia suddenly overwhelmed her senses. She turned abruptly from the scene, pushing through the onlookers.

She smacked headlong into a broad chest covered in black silk, the waft of an expensive cologne assailing her as strong hands gripped her shoulders to steady her.

"Excuse me." Kate was flustered. Master John kept his hands on her shoulders, a devilish grin on his face.

"No problem. You can slam that gorgeous body into me anytime." As his eyes caressed her body, her nipples leapt to attention beneath his gaze. She started to cover her chest with her arms, but forced herself to resist her modest impulse. She was at a play party, damn it, with a gorgeous man ogling her body. Where was the harm? It felt good to be admired.

"Like what you see, huh?" she quipped, ordering her blood to remain at bay and not color her cheeks.

"I do, indeed. I'd like to see a lot more." He let go of one of her shoulders, bringing his hand to her cheek. With two fingers, he stroked her skin, moving along her jaw to her throat. His touch caused a small shudder to ripple through her and she barely controlled the soft moan of pleasure that threatened to escape her lips.

"I'd love to scene with you," he said, his voice low and compelling. "I sense something powerful in you, Ashley. A force to be reckoned with, as yet untapped, waiting to be unleashed and tamed."

Kate's heart was beating too fast. She wasn't ready for a public scene, but her body seemed to be melting beneath his hot gaze. "I—I'm not…" Kate's mouth was dry. She swallowed, licked her lips and tried again. "I'm sorry. I'm not ready. I'm just here to watch."

Master John frowned, his eyebrows furrowing as if he were trying to comprehend what she'd said. It occurred to her he wasn't used to being refused. Why *was* she refusing the best looking guy she'd seen in years, maybe ever up close? Why was she such a chicken?

She looked away, wishing he'd stop staring at her. She felt foolish and young, out of her depth. Then the words the couple who were running the event said that morning came back to her. Any public scene should be negotiated in advance. Yes, that was her out, an out that didn't make her look like a twelve-year-old kid afraid of her first kiss.

"Maybe," she tried, "we can negotiate something for tomorrow night."

"We can negotiate right now, Ashley. I have a beautiful new cane I want to introduce to you. I can take you places you never dreamed of, little girl. Trust me." Again he lifted his hand, stroking her cheek, his touch leaving a trail of fire in its wake. Kate blew out a tremulous breath. A part of her wanted to accept his offer. She'd always been curious to feel the sting of a cane, handled by someone who knew what they were doing. But she just wasn't ready, not tonight, not in front of all these people.

"I'm sorry. I'm not ready," she said. "Not tonight."

Master John pursed his lips, something almost like anger sweeping his features for a moment so brief Kate thought she must have imagined it. Then his mouth eased into a wry smile and he shrugged. "Okay. A gentleman knows when to back off. Tomorrow then. You'll have a whole twenty-four hours to get used to the idea, and a day chock full of seminars and workshops to prepare you. Sound like a plan?"

"Yes, thank you." Kate realized she'd been tensing all the muscles in her body. All at once she relaxed, relieved she'd handled the refusal without totally closing the door on the guy.

Her attention was diverted by the piercing wail of a woman tethered spread eagle to the spider web with rope at her wrists and ankles. She was a slight woman, stark naked, her pubic mound shaven smooth. A man was striking her small breasts and thighs with a flogger, the whoosh of leather against skin audible even from a distance.

Kate gasped as the force of the blows rocked the woman in the rubber webbing. Her skin was mottled red where the leather struck, her mouth opened in a perfect O. All at once the man slapped the woman's cheek with an open palm, causing Kate's own hand to fly to her mouth. She was both upset and excited by what she was watching, her emotions pinging through her like a pinball in an arcade game.

Master John put his arm around her shoulders, and instead of shrugging away his unfamiliar touch, she leaned into him, grateful for the contact. "He slapped her," she found herself saying. "Is that okay, what they're doing?"

He squeezed gently. "Of course. For some women, face slapping is a powerful erotic trigger. It places them almost immediately in a submissive headspace. Look at her, Ashley. Look at her expression. Do you think she doesn't want what's happening to her?"

The woman's head was back now, resting against the webbing. Her lips were parted, her eyes closed, the expression on her face one of intense pleasure, almost as if she were experiencing an orgasm right in front of them, pulled from her body by the kiss of leather and the hard caress of the man's palm. Kate imagined herself there, bound and flogged, naked for all those in the room to see. She realized her own breath was shallow, and she could feel a vein pulsing at her throat. Her nipples ached and her pussy felt swollen between her legs. She leaned weakly against Master John, who held her tighter.

He spoke softly, his breath tickling her ear. "It's what she wants. It's what she needs. You understand that. I know you do. It's why you're here, Ashley. It's why you're watching tonight. It's why you'll be participating tomorrow night. Just like her, you need to feel the pain to find the pleasure, the ultimate pleasure of surrender."

Kate opened her mouth to refute him, but no words came.

~*~

"I'm sorry, what?"

Chase realized Justin had been saying something, but he'd zoned out, thinking about *her*.

"Chase, what the hell is the matter with you, man? You're off somewhere in the ozone tonight. If I didn't know better, I'd say you were in love."

Chase glanced sharply at his friend. "Yeah, right."

His voice must have come out more harshly than he intended, because Justin's face crumpled into an apology. "Hey, I'm sorry. I didn't mean..."

"No, no. Nothing to be sorry about. If anyone's sorry, it's me. You're right. I'm distracted tonight."

Justin nodded sympathetically and took a long swig of his beer. Chase knew Justin assumed he was in one of those funks, brooding over Lisa, but tonight at least, that wasn't the case.

He was thinking about Ashley, the bewitching girl who'd sat front and center at his bondage seminar, her long, lovely legs tucked up under her, those emerald green eyes sparkling at him when she smiled.

He realized with a start that until this evening he hadn't even thought about another woman since Lisa. What had it been now...a year? Was a heart he was sure had been shattered beyond repair actually showing some signs of life?

It probably had less to do with his heart and more to do with his dick, he told himself. Though that in itself was something. The curve of her soft cheek had so distracted him, he'd nearly forgotten how to tie a simple square knot. All that wavy copper hair and long, lean limbs. She was elegant, yet something in her face was innocent, almost yearning. He had gotten the sense she was new to the scene, but eager. His cock stirred at the thought of introducing her to sensual bondage.

Oddly, she was nothing like Lisa, who was dark and petite with a smile, the rare times she bestowed it on him, that could melt a glacier. He'd prided himself on winning those smiles, delighted when he could make her happy, even if the happiness was fleeting. If only he could have done something more, been something more. If only his love had been enough.

Chase was distracted from his musings by Justin punching him quite hard on the arm. "Ouch. What was that for?" Chase rubbed the bruised muscle.

"You're lost in space again, my friend. Maybe you need to call it a night."

"Man, I'm sorry." Chase ran his hands over his face and up through his hair. "Maybe you're right." He looked at his watch. It was nearly ten. The play party would just be getting started.

Chase never attended BDSM play parties, at least he hadn't in a long time. Lisa had enjoyed them, and to humor her he would sometimes take her, but as a rule they weren't his style. Most of the folks, or so it seemed to him, were players and posers, putting on a show for each other and themselves. He supposed that was fine, as far as it went, but for Chase, D/s mattered too much. He didn't want to put it up on parade.

He paid his tab and left Justin at the pub. Fortunately there was a table of guys nearby they both knew, and Justin moved off to join them.

Chase began to walk toward the subway station that would take him to Queens, but instead found himself passing it by. He was headed, he realized, for the converted warehouse where the Power Play party was taking place. Maybe he'd just walk by, see if the lights were on upstairs. After all, he'd see Ashley tomorrow. Maybe she'd sign up for his Shibari workshop, and he'd convince her to volunteer. Maybe he'd get there early enough this time for the breakfast, and just happen to find himself standing next to her.

Yes, better just to call it a night, as Justin suggested. He had a good book by Walter Mosley waiting to be read, and a bottle of Heineken with his name on it.

His feet ignored his brain, walking on toward the SoHo neighborhood that housed the dungeon. The doors to the old warehouse were locked, a wise precaution, but happily, Chase had a key, courtesy of M&M.

He used it, entering the place and locking the door behind him. Upstairs was empty. He could hear the sound of music below, punctuated by the occasional crack of leather and sharp cry. Was she down there now, bound to the web, or chained to a whipping post, those long legs bare, arms lifted high overhead?

He moved quietly down the stairs and stood at the bottom, letting his eyes adjust to the dim light. After a moment he spotted her, and was both relieved to see she wasn't actively participating in a scene, and annoyed to see that she wasn't alone. John Brighton was with her. They stood in profile, John's arm proprietarily around her, leaning down to murmur something as they watched a scene.

Though Chase barely knew the woman, he couldn't help the barb of jealousy that hooked into his heart. For some stupid reason, he'd hoped she'd have more sense than to associate with that poser.

Though he knew that wasn't fair. Most people in the scene liked Brighton, or at least respected him. Women were blinded by his pretty boy good looks and charming manner, but Chase had his doubts. He'd watched Brighton scene a few times, taking his women to the brink of nonconsensual play in a way that had disturbed Chase on more than one occasion. He'd even broached the subject once with the guy, and had been dismayed by his response.

"She wanted it, Saunders. They're all the same, these sub girls. They say, 'no, no, stop, please,' but they want you to beat the shit out of them. Trust me. I know women." He'd placed a subtle emphasis on the word "I", as if to imply that Chase didn't. Even worse, in Chase's estimation, was the sneer in his voice, the evident lack of respect toward the women who put their trust in him in a way Chase viewed as sacred.

That was the only time Brighton had shown what Chase believed were his true colors, but he'd never trusted the guy after that. And now the bastard had his hooks into Ashley, who Chase was pretty sure was way out of her league. He felt an urge to protect her, to rush over and push Brighton's arm from her shoulders, to warn her. Of course he did no such thing. She was a grown woman, and one he knew next to nothing about, other than that she was the first woman since Lisa who had piqued his interest. It was just his own jealousy talking, he told himself. She could take care of herself. Her choices were her own.

Aware he would have been better off never having shown up, he turned away, dispirited, and climbed the stairs. In the thirty seconds he'd stood in shadows no one had seen him and that, at least, was a good thing. He'd go home, get a good night's sleep and see what tomorrow held. After all, if John could make a bid for the girl, so could he.

Whoa. Where had that come from? Was he ready to leap back into the fray, just like that? Was a pretty smile and sparkling eyes really all it took? Lisa loomed into his mind, bringing with her the familiar aura of guilt and regret. But instead of embracing the feelings, wrapping them like a hair shirt around his heart as he'd done for so long, tonight, with a supreme act of will, he shrugged them away.

By the time he came outside into the warm evening air, Chase felt a little better. Coppery hair, green eyes, the curve of a breast—that's all he really knew of this woman called Ashley. He knew nothing of her mind or heart. Yet, though he'd probably already lost her to Brighton, he recognized that his attraction to her was in itself a good thing.

Though Lisa was gone, Chase found himself ready, just maybe, to begin to feel again. After all, at thirty-five, he was still a man with appetites and desires, and the world was waiting for him to rejoin it. Forcing a bounce to his step, Chase walked away, jingling the change in his pocket and whistling. He was alive, and life, while not always easy, was good.

Chapter 4

Stacey poured brandy into the plastic cups she'd found in the motel bathroom and handed one across the narrow space between their two beds. Kate took it and sipped.

It was nearly two in the morning. Both women were dressed for bed, Kate in her favorite pink cotton nightgown, Stacey in a black lacy camisole and matching panties. "I got this new just for the weekend," she'd commented when she came out of the bathroom. "In case I got lucky."

"Weekend's not over yet." Kate smiled, wondering if she too would get lucky. Wondering if she had the nerve to find out.

"That's the only bad thing about these BDSM events," Stacey said, taking a sizable gulp from her cup. "No alcohol at the play parties."

"I guess a drunk guy with a whip in his hand isn't the best idea," Kate offered.

"Yeah, I know. But I look better the more my partner drinks." Stacey laughed. She finished off her drink and poured herself another. "So, what'd you think? Did you have fun being the voyeur?"

"It was quite a show, I have to admit," Kate replied. "Kind of sensory overload after a while, watching all those different scenes going on."

"Well, you should have participated in one. When you're in the zone, all of that background noise just disappears. It's only about you and your Dom then. What he's doing, and how you're responding."

Kate nodded, thinking about Victor. They'd had fun as far as it went, but she'd never achieved the sort of sublime serenity she'd read about in her research. Would she ever find that? Did she want to? Stacey was watching her, apparently expecting a response, so Kate said vaguely, "It's been a long time for me."

Stacey tilted her head. "I kind of got that feeling. You're not a total novice to the scene, but certainly not a regular." She held out the brandy bottle. Kate drank the rest of hers and held out her cup, her eyes watering from the strong liquor.

As they each settled back against their pillows, Stacey said, "So what's your story? What do you do to make ends meet?" Stacey patted her teased hair, which she'd covered with a net scarf for the night. "As you probably guessed, I'm a hair and makeup artist. I work for a very chic salon in Brooklyn."

Kate didn't comment on this, instead swallowing more brandy. The liquor was spreading nicely through her body now, easing along her limbs with a satisfying warmth. Why not tell Stacey the truth? After all, Kate was proud of her work. "I'm a writer. I write erotic romance novels. Quit my day job two years ago and never looked back."

"Wow, how cool is that?" Stacey enthused. "You got any with you? Give me a signed copy. How many books you got out? What's your full name? Ashley…"

"Ashley Kendall. But that's my pen name. My real name is Kate. Kate Alexander." Now what in hell had made her admit that? She was supposed to be incognito! Oh well, Stacey was nice and sweet, and it was fun to share secrets with a girlfriend. It had been ages since she had, she realized. It felt good to connect with someone, however fleeting the connection.

"Kate." Stacey nodded. "That name suits you much better. Why the secrecy?"

Kate shrugged. "I don't know. I don't usually make a habit of going to BDSM weekends…"

"So? No law against them. You're not doing anything wrong."

Kate was silent, realizing a part of her must hold at least some of Victor's assertions that BDSM was perverse—a deviant behavior that had to be hidden, denied and kept in check. Maybe that's why she hadn't made any attempt during the two years that had passed to find another partner with the same kink. This realization bothered her.

"I was with a guy, Victor," she said, aware her tongue was probably being loosened by the brandy. "This was two years ago. It was the first time I ever did anything with bondage and erotic pain and all. I'd always had fantasies of a dominant man taking control, but I'd pretty much rejected them as not worthy of a strong, independent woman.

"At first he was into it. He liked the ropes and the sexy little outfits he got for me to wear. It was an exciting, naughty game. When I brought home a flogger and a riding crop, he started freaking out. I wanted to go further than he did, I guess. I wanted to press the envelope more, experience more than just a sexy game."

She shrugged sadly. "He did this one-eighty on me. Told me I was a sicko, and he'd just gone along with the games in order to try to salvage a failing relationship. The ironic thing was, he was right, in a way. Our relationship had been kind of faltering, and the BDSM play gave us something new to focus on, to try. But in the end it wasn't enough."

"Two years!" Stacey exploded. "You haven't played in two years? We have got to fix this situation, pronto. You aren't leaving this weekend until you've done a scene. A real scene with a real Dom."

Kate smiled, immediately thinking of Master John and his proposal. "Yeah, okay. We'll see."

"Yes, we will, missy. Might as well get used to the idea, because it's happening."

Kate drank the last of her brandy and nestled into the pillows, closing her eyes. Maybe Stacey was right. Maybe it was time to experience what she craved. Why not tomorrow at the party? What, after all, did she have to lose?

~*~

Chase arrived early the next morning, in time for the breakfast. He'd already consumed three cups of coffee and eaten a Danish he hadn't really wanted, cornered most of the time by a couple of bondage enthusiasts, when she finally appeared.

She looked even lovelier than the day before, wearing a silky sky blue sundress, matching sandals on her pretty feet, her long, shapely legs bare. He waited while she got herself some coffee and a bagel, feeling for all the world like he was fourteen again and trying to get up the courage to ask a girl to the school dance.

"Good morning," he said, approaching her. She stood with Stacey and a couple Chase recognized as Amber and William, both active players in the scene. He joined the group, engaging in their small talk, wondering how or when he could get her alone.

While William was telling Chase how much he'd enjoyed the suspension bondage workshop, Brighton suddenly appeared, wearing a muscle T-shirt over his sculpted torso, flashing a white smile of greeting, his eyes raking Ashley with an insolent stare.

Pleasantries were again exchanged, and a few of last night's scenes discussed. "I didn't see you there last night," Ashley said, turning her pretty smile toward Chase, who couldn't help but smile back.

"Saunders doesn't do public play parties," Brighton announced, speaking for him and heartily annoying Chase in the process.

Hiding his annoyance, Chase focused on Ashley. "Actually I do from time to time. In fact, I was thinking of coming tonight. I'd be delighted to show you some sensual bondage positions we didn't get a chance to review at the workshop. I have some beautiful new rope I made myself. Soft as satin against your skin, but strong as steel."

"Ashley's not interested in bondage. She's aching to feel the satisfying sting of my cane, aren't you?" Brighton interrupted, his eyes on Ashley.

She looked flustered, a spot of red appearing on each soft cheek. "Oh, I, uh, I haven't really decided if I'm even going to — "

"Oh, you're going to, all right," Stacey interrupted, her round face creasing into a broad grin. "Remember our talk. You promised."

Chase could see Ashley was feeling put on the spot, and hated to think he'd been a part of that. "Okay guys," he said. "We can all back off now. It's not good etiquette to pressure someone to do a scene. I'm sure we all agree on that," he added pointedly, glaring at Brighton. He refused to compete with the guy for a scene with Ashley, as if she were an object to be won. Turning back to her, he said, "We can talk about this later. No need to make decisions now. If you decide to do a scene tonight, it's got to be your decision, based on your desires and expectations, not someone else's."

Ashley nodded and flashed him a grateful smile. Chase felt as if she'd reached right in and squeezed his heart. He put his hand lightly on her bare shoulder, unprepared for the electrical current of raw desire that shot through him when he touched her. He withdrew his hand, hoping his voice was steady. Jesus, was he losing his mind?

"I'll hook up with you later, okay?" he said, avoiding the curious stares of Stacey, William and Amber, and the knowing leer of that bastard, Brighton.

~*~

Kate was sitting in one of the folding chairs in front of the stage, waiting for the seminar on discipline and correction in a Master/slave relationship put on by a speaker she hadn't heard yet. She figured she'd get some good information there for her novel, if nothing else.

Stacey had opted to nap instead, after extracting a promise from Kate that she'd agree to a scene with *someone*. "You could do worse than Chase," Stacey had advised, once they were alone. "He's hot in his own quiet way, and really knows his way around a piece of rope. Now, Master John..." Stacey caressed the words, stroked them. "John..." she said again, a dreamy expression on her face. "Shit, he's so good looking you almost don't care if he knows what he's doing or not, you know? Man, I could eat that guy with a spoon. No, forget the spoon!" She laughed, but added, "Seriously, though, Chase is right. It's your choice. Must be nice to have two guys fighting over you. Maybe if I lost fifty pounds, they'd be fighting over me."

Speaking of the devil, Master John suddenly appeared, settling into the empty seat beside Kate. "Hey," he said, putting his hand lightly on her thigh. "Fancy meeting you here."

"Hi," she answered, looking down at his hand on her thigh. He removed it, brushing his fingers along her skin as he did, his eyes hooding.

"So, you given thought to your scene tonight? You ready to experience the raw power of a sensual caning? I'll take you slowly, building your tolerance for the sting until you're begging for more. Would you like that, Ashley? Would you like to feel the erotic sting of my cane?"

Kate swallowed, aroused by his words. Yes, she wanted it, but she was afraid. If only she knew him better. If only it didn't have to be in a public venue, with people watching...

"Are you afraid?" he asked softly, as if listening in on her thoughts.

"Yes," she admitted, looking into his handsome face.

"It's okay. A little fear is a good thing. It heightens the experience. Trust me. I know what you need. I'll teach you what it is to suffer and soar with ecstasy. With me you'll find the Master that until now you only dreamed of." He put his hand again on her thigh. Kate found herself suppressing the urge to laugh at his pompous words. But at the same time, she couldn't deny the thrill of desire sparking through her from his touch.

~*~

"It's better this way," Chase tried to tell himself. "You don't do public scenes. You can get her number. You can call her sometime, ask her out for a drink. Get to know her the right way. Your way."

Though he knew this was wise advice, and the right course, he had a hard time swallowing the bile of jealousy and lost opportunity rising in his throat. As he'd feared, Brighton had gotten to Ashley before he had, and talked her into a scene.

Chase finally managed to get a few moments alone with Ashley. Aware it might sound like sour grapes, but feeling a certain responsibility for a woman who didn't really seem to know what she was getting herself into, he had gently asked her about her experience with canes and erotic pain in general.

"I've had enough to know what I want," she'd retorted, taking offense where none was meant.

He'd felt a fool, but had persisted, "Okay. Just be careful. Brighton, er, Master John, has a reputation for being a little, uh, intense. I just want to caution you to follow your own instincts. If you're not comfortable with what's happening, speak up. There's no dishonor in using your safeword either, if you need it. Okay?"

She'd looked frightened at that remark, and he'd backpedaled, embarrassed to be putting his nose where it wasn't invited—after all, he barely knew this woman. She might be the biggest pain slut in the place for all he knew.

But no, his intuition told him otherwise, and his intuition was rarely wrong, especially as it pertained to submissive women. It wasn't something he bragged about, or even thought about that much, but he had a knack, an ability to listen to their bodies, to gauge their reactions and cues even before they spoke, especially during D/s play. Ashley was eager, interested and completely inexperienced. A caning scene with John Brighton was not the ideal way to introduce her to the pleasures of erotic pain, of that he was pretty sure.

Oh well. She hadn't consulted him on the matter. She'd chosen Brighton over him, and that was that. He glanced at his watch. Eight o'clock. He turned on the shower in the bathroom of his small but comfortable house in Queens. He would shave and dress and return for the party.

He would attend as a kind of back up for Ashley. One thing he could do was be around. Just in case she got in a little over her head. He'd be there for her — her safe place if things got a little crazy, as they sometimes did at these play parties.

That wasn't the only reason he was going. In the back of his mind, he realized he was actually considering a public scene with her. He could imagine her bound in his ropes, suspended in a bondage swing, her body offered for him to touch, to taste, to explore.

For the first time since Lisa, his blood was thrumming, his bruised heart beating with the pulse of a new desire. Something about Ashley had got hold of him, and he couldn't shake it.

When he'd seen her in that little sundress, he wanted to pull down the narrow straps from her shoulders. He wanted to see her dress drop at her feet in a puddle, and watch her step out of it, standing tall and proud, offering her body to him.

He wanted to trace his tongue along the curve of her throat, and pull her close to feel the sweetness of her skin, the soft touch of her lips. He would kiss her lightly at first, his lips just grazing hers. He wanted to feel the moment her hand moved beneath the cotton of his shirt when she touched, for the very first time, the skin of his body. He wanted her to kneel submissively at his feet, lifting her chin, parting her lips, eager for his cock, for his offering, for his taking what was his.

He wanted to hear the sounds that came from her throat when she had no breath left, when she was breathless with desire. He wanted to possess her, to enter her bloodstream like a drug, like a rush of ecstasy.

His cock was erect with desire for a woman beyond his reach. He was powerless now, the wheels of a scene with another guy already set in motion. He felt like the enchanted frog in a fairy tale, watching while his princess kissed the wrong guy. Loneliness moved like fire beneath his skin. Closing his eyes, he lifted his face to the water, almost wishing he'd never laid eyes on her.

~*~

"I really can't believe I let you talk me into this." Kate preened in front of the mirror, turning this way and that in her black satin waist cincher. She'd drawn the line at the skintight miniskirt Stacey had tried to convince her to get at the Village fetish shop where they'd bought the cincher. Instead she'd opted for a sheer white skirt that fell in lush folds to mid-calf. It was sexy without being too revealing. Beneath it she wore white thigh highs with lace tops. Though Stacey had encouraged her to go without, Kate had insisted on the black lace thong as well.

"I like the effect," Stacey pronounced. "The dark and the light, the naughty and the pure. You're like halfway between an angel and a whore."

"Every man's dream, right?" Kate laughed to hide her nervousness. She could hardly believe this was happening. She was going to scene with Master John! God, what if she messed up? Wimped out? Chase's advice had unnerved her.

"You know," she said, turning to Stacey. "Chase Saunders kind of warned me to watch out with Master John. Said he could get a little intense. I think that's the word he used."

Stacey laughed. "Consider the source. He's jealous. He made a bid for you and lost. Sure he's gonna trash the other guy. A sort of 'I told you' kind of thing in advance." Stacey rubbed her hands together and waggled her eyebrows. "Anyway, intense is *good*. It's perfect for sensation junkies. That's what we are, you know, or what any masochistic sub girl worth her salt is—a sensation junkie. Mere pleasure is not enough. We crave the feel of being restrained, the added thrill of the pain. And trust me, Master John will give you all that and more."

"That," Kate admitted, hugging herself, "is what I'm afraid of."

"A little fear," Stacey said, unconsciously echoing Master John's earlier assertion, "is a good thing."

Chapter 5

Stacey abandoned Kate nearly the moment they entered the dungeon. Two tall, good looking men had invited Stacey and Kate to join a scene with them that involved an electric bondage board and a cattle prod. Stacey agreed immediately, while Kate demurred, relieved she had the ready excuse of a scene with Master John.

"Too bad you're already busy," Stacey said with a wink. "Nothing like a few jolts to get the heart going."

Left alone, Kate saw Chase Saunders arrive, looking sort of out of place in his faded blue jeans, though at least this time his shirt was black. She started to go over and say hi, but was distracted by Master John, who appeared suddenly in front of her.

He was wearing a white linen shirt open at the throat, the skin tan beneath it. Black leather pants that look soft as butter molded to his legs and muscular ass. Kate tried not to stare at the sexy bulge at his crotch.

"Like what you see?" Master John's eyes were half closed, one side of his mouth lifted slightly in an amused, almost condescending smile. Kate tried to come up with a snappy comeback, but she was too nervous to think on her feet.

Instead she offered. "We're opposites. You're white on black, I'm black on white." She twirled, making her skirt billow as she offered a nervous smile.

He reached out, stroking her collarbone with one finger. "You look ravishing. It's going to take every ounce of self-control I possess not to rip that bodice off you. But that skirt." He fingered the gauzy fabric, lifting and letting it fall. "Entirely too much material. I can't possibly cane you properly with all that in the way. That's not what we negotiated, Ashley." There was a hint of reproach in his voice.

They had agreed to a bare-bottomed caning. There was so much nudity and near-nudity all around them, Kate knew she was silly to even give it a second thought, but she couldn't help it. She wasn't used to stripping for someone she'd just met, and especially not in a public venue, even if no one around them batted an eye.

"You can lift the skirt in back," she informed him, aware she sounded prim, but ready to defend her decision if he protested.

Instead, he tilted his head to one side, appraising her with those deep, difficult to read eyes. He nodded slowly. "Agreed. Let me show you our space. I have a special area reserved. Very private. No gawking crowd."

Kate was glad to hear this. Though she was excited and even eager to experience the cane for the first time, she hadn't relished the idea of a bunch of guys leering at her. She followed Master John to a far corner of the dungeon, moving past various scenes already in play, wondering where in the room Stacey was and if she was having fun.

Master John led her to an area at the far corner of the dungeon, closed off by several tall sectioned wooden screens. He moved one of the screens and gestured for her to enter the enclosed area.

A long wooden bar, not unlike a ballet dancer's bar, had been bolted into one wall at waist height. There were two sets of handcuffs attached to the bar, one cuff of each pair secured around it, the other open, a small silver key attached. A single light hung overhead from a chord, calling to Kate's mind an interrogation room in some old spy film. The walls were concrete, bare and gray, but the floor, at least, had been covered with a thick throw rug.

Kate stood in the center of the small enclosed area, hugging herself. She felt unsure and very nervous. She was attracted to Master John, and she wanted to feel the cane, but she found herself wondering if maybe she had been moving too fast, caught up in the dynamic of the event, where everyone around her seemed to leap into play with barely a thought.

Perhaps Master John sensed her nervousness, because he moved to stand in front of her and reached out to take her into his arms. He didn't try to kiss her, for which she was relieved. Instead he just held her for several long moments, his arms strong and comforting around her. She leaned against him, closing her eyes.

He spoke in a low, soothing voice. "Here's what's going to happen, Ashley. When I let you go, you're going to walk over to the bar and grip it with both hands. I'm going to cuff your wrists in place. The cuffs are regulation metal police cuffs, but they've been lined with lambs' wool to protect your skin. They will tighten though, if you jerk too hard against them.

"I think you'll find being restrained makes it easier to handle the cane. You're not tempted to reach back and protect yourself. A natural instinct but one that could result in damage, since hands and arms don't have the nice protective padding your ass has.

"I'll start slow. I'll work you up to it. I'll take you where you've been longing to go." He released her from his embrace, holding her a moment by the shoulders as he stared into her eyes. His voice took on a deep, oratorical tone. "Are you ready, slave girl? Ready to submit to my erotic control? Ready to experience the touch of a true Master?"

As had happened before when he talked like this, Kate found herself stifling an urge to giggle. He was handsome, he was sexy, he was offering what she thought she wanted, but though she hated to admit it, the guy was a little too stuck on himself.

"Is something amusing you?" Master John frowned, the annoyance evident in his tone.

The giggle burst out in a gush of nervous laughter, which only served to irritate the guy further. His frown turned into a glower. "I'm *very* selective about who I scene with. If this is just a game to you—" he began.

"No, I'm sorry," she apologized, cutting him off. "It's just—you're just…" How did she say it without offending him? *You're really hot, but you're a pompous ass?* After all, what did she really know about protocol in the scene? Maybe all so-called Masters talked like characters out of a poorly written porn novel. What did she know?

And yeah, maybe he was a little full of himself, but at least he knew what he was doing. After all, he was a professional. He gave seminars and workshops on the art of whipping. And they were just doing a scene, not getting engaged.

"I'm sorry," she tried again. "Just nerves."

The thunder eased out of his face. His eyebrows returned to their normal position over his eyes and he nodded, apparently accepting her excuse. "Okay then. You ready?"

Kate nodded.

"Then do what I said. Take hold of the bar. I'm going to cuff your wrists."

Kate moved toward the wall, her heart fluttering. She gripped the bar, which was polished and smooth, glad for something to hold onto. Master John moved behind her, coming up so close she could feel the heat of his body. He reached first for her left wrist, locking it, though he left the key in place. The lambs' wool lining made it soft, and there was room to maneuver her wrist, if she felt the need.

He secured the second cuff. The metallic click ratcheted the beat of her heart from flutter to pounding and she found herself breathing too fast. It was happening. There was no backing out now.

He pulled her hair back, tucking it behind her ears. "Slow your breathing," he said. "We haven't even started yet. Take in a deep breath and hold it." She obeyed. "That's better," he continued. "Now let it out, slowly. We aren't going to start until you're ready."

Kate nodded. *See*, she told herself, *he's a pro. Relax. The guy knows what he's doing.* She focused on her breathing — deep in…slow out. Deep in…slow out. After a while she did feel herself calming down. Her heart had slowed to a more normal pace and she could catch her breath.

"Much better," Master John pronounced. "Are you ready, slave girl? I want to start the scene. That means you obey me, to the letter. You do what I say, you take what I give you. Understood?"

Kate nodded, her heart picking up its pace despite the relaxation techniques just employed. She would use this experience for her novel. It would be set in ancient Rome. The girl had been a princess in her own realm, before it was conquered and absorbed by Rome. Now she was just a slave girl, a part of the spoils of war. She had been sold to a powerful man with dangerous sexual appetites who had the authority to have her put to death if she didn't obey his every whim. The setting would be lush, draped in silk, scented with perfumes and incense, ripe with erotic danger and sexual promise…

"Step back and kick off your shoes." Master John's voice pulled Kate back to the moment. "I want you to bend forward, ass out, legs shoulder-width apart. Keep your face forward, head down." Kate swallowed hard as she moved to obey. This was no fiction. It was real.

He moved behind her. She could hear the unzipping of something—probably his duffel bag. A moment later he appeared at her side. She turned to look at him. He was holding a long, thin cane with a dark wooden handle. He whipped it in the air a few times, which made her flinch and bite her lip.

His smile was cruel, his eyes sparkling. "That's right. Soon you'll feel that on your ass. On this beautiful ass." He bent slightly, reaching beneath her long skirt, running his hand along her leg until he was cupping one cheek. The thong Kate was wearing did little to cover her bottom, save for the strip of black lace between the cheeks. She held her breath as his hand moved over her skin, lightly stroking the flesh. She half-feared, half-ached for his hand to move lower, between her legs.

Instead he lifted her skirt, bunching and twisting it in his hands before tucking it into its waistband. She felt the cool air against her ass and legs. "I don't like that look," he announced. "The skirt all bunched up like that is very unattractive. Visuals are so important in the scene, Ashley. Surely you can appreciate that."

She said nothing, but shifted slightly, feeling the slight tug of the cuffs around her wrists. As she moved, the gathered skirt came loose, falling again over her legs. Master John gave an annoyed snort.

"It won't do. This will end up being a liability. It could get in the way and I could harm you without meaning to." He moved close behind her again, pressing his body against hers. He brought his arms around her, enfolding her from behind. He smelled good and his hard body felt good pressed against hers.

She pressed back against him, letting a small sigh escape her lips. Taking her cue, he nuzzled her neck, lightly kissing the skin. "Let me take it off," he murmured. "It's not like you're exposing anything more than tucking it up would do." He kissed her again, the tip of his tongue drawing a line along her flesh.

He was right. If she trusted him to cuff and cane her, surely it was okay to remove her skirt. She nodded her assent. Master John stepped back at once, letting her go. She wanted him back. If she hadn't been cuffed to the bar, she would have turned around and pulled him into her arms.

She was, she suddenly realized, very lonely for physical touch. She hadn't been out on a date for months, so caught up in her work, and anyway, there was no one she knew in whom she had the slightest interest. That was one of the disadvantages of country living — the pickings were slim.

Master John unbuttoned and unzipped the skirt, letting it fall to her feet. She stepped aside, allowing him to whisk it away. She still had the waist cincher, which effectively covered her body. Its tight grip was comforting somehow, like a man's hands spanning her waist.

"Beautiful," Master John murmured, the appreciation ripe in his voice. In spite of herself, Kate couldn't stop the small smile his compliment pulled from her. He cupped the globes of her ass and then ran his fingers lightly along her inner thighs, stroking the bare skin above the lace bands of her stockings. Kate shifted slightly, willing his hands to move higher, her heart thumping fast. Following her silent dictate, Master John's hands moved up, the fingers grazing the throbbing pulse at her sex.

"You want this, don't you?" he whispered. "I can feel your heat." She held herself very still, her heart thudding in her ears. They hadn't negotiated any sex for this scene, but touching wasn't sex, was it? And anyway, she wanted it. He was right. She *needed* it. She needed his touch.

"Oh!" The word was pulled involuntarily from her lips when she felt him pulling aside the lace that covered her swollen labia. His fingers moved feather-light over the delicate folds and Kate shuddered. Her face was hot with a mixture of lust and embarrassment, but she didn't want him to stop.

He pushed the tip of one finger into her entrance and gave a low growl of muted laughter. "Yes, you're wet. Sopping. Of course you are. You were born to be displayed for my pleasure, to experience the erotic suffering that can take you places you never dreamed."

This time she felt no urge to giggle at his words. They struck a chord deep inside her. Yes, she was born to this. It felt so *right*. It felt right that her wrists were tethered, her ass bared, her legs spread, waiting to feel the kiss of the cane, the stroke of strong, masculine fingers moving over her skin. She sighed and arched her back, literally aching for his touch.

Master John withdrew his hand and Kate suppressed a sigh. *Down, girl,* she told herself, reminding herself she wasn't here to have sex, but to experience a caning firsthand. If something developed later between them, well and good.

Master John drew the cane along her skin. "Are you ready, lovely girl? Ready to suffer for me?" The words sent another tremor through her. Erotic suffering, a concept she understood intellectually but had never fully grasped. How could pain equal pleasure? And yet she was longing to find out. She ached to know, at last, what it was she'd been yearning for and had yet to find. She'd been waiting for this for so long. Victor had tried, but failed to give her what she needed.

Had she found it at last with this man?

"Yes," she whispered. "I'm ready."

She startled as she heard the whoosh of bamboo whipping through the air beside her. But when the cane touched her skin, the stroke was light, not at all painful. It was more of a tap. He moved it over both cheeks and the backs of her thighs, keeping up a steady tap-tap-tap that warmed her skin but didn't hurt a bit.

He kept this up for some time, until she almost asked him to do it harder. She wanted to feel its fiery sting. She was ready. As if reading her mind, he increased the stroke's power, just enough.

He reached again between her legs, his fingers moving over the lace, which Kate realized was wet with her own juices. He tugged at it, pulling the fabric up between her labia and then drawing his fingers along the exposed, swollen flesh on either side. Kate's clit was throbbing and she came within a hair's breadth of begging him to make her come.

Instead, his hand was again withdrawn, moving over her ass cheeks, preparing it for what she knew was to come—what she wanted, she reminded herself, far more than a simple orgasm.

This time, he used more of the cane, letting it lick in long, stinging lines over both cheeks at once. It hurt, yes, it did, but it was a good pain, if that made any sense. It darted along her nerve endings, zinging straight toward her sex.

As he continued to flick the bamboo, slowly but steadily increasing the intensity, Kate began to breathe faster, clenching the bar to keep still. He struck harder, one slicing cut that made her gasp and instinctively close her legs.

"Back into position." Master John punctuated his command with several stinging strokes to her thighs. Kate hurried to obey, her heart now slamming into her ribs. He struck her ass again, even harder than before, and again she gasped, jerking against the bar, though she managed to keep her legs apart.

"It hurts. Too much," she managed between pants. What had just a moment before been a perfect balance between pleasure and erotic suffering now shifted decidedly toward pure pain. Why had she thought she wanted this? Yet, even as this thought entered her mind, her skin was tingling, waiting, anticipating the next fiery stroke.

"It hurts just enough," Master John countered. "And you're only just beginning. You won't be laughing at me when we're done, I assure you, little girl."

"Oh, no," she protested. "I wasn't laughing at you. I was just—" Her words ended in yet another gasp as his cane caught her sharply across her left cheek, its tip curling cruelly against her hip.

"I know exactly what you were doing. It's one reason I choose beautiful women to subjugate." Something in his voice had changed—hardened. Kate was confused by the sudden shift in mood. The air itself felt chillier. "Beneath the soft skin, pretty smiles and perky tits, you're all just dirty cunts who need to be put in their place. You need taming. You need humbling.

You haven't learned that a woman's place is naked at a man's feet. You have to be taught." His words were like ice on her skin.

He struck her again, several times in rapid succession. "Ow, ow, ow!" Kate was dancing on her feet, trying in vain to move away from the sharp bite of the bamboo. Her wrists were caught painfully now in the grip of the cuffs, which had tightened as she jerked away. She tried to process what the hell he'd just said, while her body sought to avoid the cane. She didn't like the sneering tone that had crept into his voice. She liked the words he'd said even less. *You're all just dirty cunts.* What the fuck...?

"Hush." His voice was sharp. "You're too loud. I'll gag you if you don't quiet down."

Panic edged her words. "John, please. I need to slow down."

"That's *Master* John. You forget yourself, slave girl. I'll decide when you need to slow down, not you." He struck her again, just as hard.

"Please! I can't..." She panted, trying to catch her breath. "You're going too fast. It's too much. I've never—"

He clamped his hand suddenly over her mouth, his fingers pressing painfully hard against her cheek. He leaned down, his lips close to her ear. "Don't give me that crap. You can protest all you want, but your cunt doesn't lie. You love it. You're a pain slut, just like all of them. You need the pain. You beg and plead for me to stop, but you know you want it. Deal with it. Embrace it. I'm not going to stop until *I* decide you've had enough." His body was pressed against hers and she could feel his erection, an iron bar poking hard against her back.

The first gush of real fear exploded inside her. Adrenaline shot through her blood and she felt dizzy, almost sick. His hand was still clamped on her mouth, but she managed to nod. The minute he took his hand off, she'd say her safeword. She'd scream it. Though she hadn't been sure what to expect, this wasn't it. This scene needed to end. Now.

But when he let go, he used the cane so quickly she didn't have time to speak, as it caught her like a blade across both thighs. The explosion of pain left her voiceless for several seconds, all the air smacked out of her by the sudden, vicious cut of his cane.

"Fuck," she finally whispered, her eyes squeezed tight. He struck her again, a second line of stinging fire.

"No," she moaned. She knew she was supposed to be saying something else, but for the moment all coherent thought had vanished from her mind.

Biting cut after biting cut of the cane moved over her thighs and ass like hornets stinging in long, agonizing lines. There was nothing erotic anymore in what was happening. It was a beating, plain and simple.

Red.

She just had to say that word. Just force her lips, tongue and breath to cooperate… *Help me.*

"Red," she finally managed, her voice a ragged whisper. He didn't seem to hear her, or if he had, he ignored it. The caning went on. She felt herself sagging against the railing as her knees gave way. Pain spilled through her mind like blood gushing from a wound, blotting everything but the desire to escape. Dimly, she was aware of a low, feral moan. It was, she finally realized with vague horror, her own voice.

Chapter 6

Chase saw Ashley, red shiny hair cascading over a black corset and loose flowing white skirt, and his heart constricted. He started toward her, drawn like a moth to her flame. As luck would have it, John Brighton chose that moment to appear, causing Chase to halt in his tracks.

He watched them talk a few minutes, and then Brighton led Ashley toward the back of the dungeon, no doubt to one of the secluded play areas where onlookers weren't welcome.

Chase wanted to follow them. He wanted to keep tabs on Ashley. No, what he really wanted was to be the one leading her by the hand, though not toward a play area, but out of the building. They could go for a drink and talk. He could find out about her—what she did, what her interest in BDSM was, if she had someone significant waiting at home. He could stare into those lovely green eyes and lean forward to kiss her soft, red lips…

Chase was distracted from his musings by Amber and William, who were waving wildly as they approached him. William was hefting a large messenger bag over his shoulder that Chase guessed was filled with ropes, chain and other paraphernalia for their evening of public play and display.

"Chase!" William enthused when they were close enough to speak. "I am so glad we ran into you. I didn't think you came to the parties."

Chase shrugged. "Not usually." He didn't elaborate.

"Well, it's great you're here now. I've got these cool new suspension cuffs for hanging Amber upside down by her ankles. A bunch of guys are going to take turns flogging her."

"I can't *wait*," Amber burst in, her smile wide. She was a pretty woman, petite with honey blond hair, decked out in a red leather mini dress that exposed more than it covered.

William nodded enthusiastically. "It'd be great if you could check out the rope rigging for me. We wouldn't want Amber to fall on her head."

Not able to think of a polite way to refuse, Chase followed the couple, his mind still on Ashley and Brighton. It was a good twenty minutes before he could finally extricate himself from the pair. He told himself it was a good thing he'd helped them, as William had chosen the wrong rope for the project, and was barely competent at knots, despite attending a number of Chase's seminars and hands-on workshops. How he'd managed to avoid harming Amber to this point was anybody's guess.

Chase moved slowly through the dungeon, his progress impeded on several more occasions by folks surprised to see him there, or eager for a bit of advice for their bondage scenes. He spied Stacey with two tall, good looking guys. They had her on her back between them, legs spread wide, some kind of board with electrodes attached to it secured at her crotch. Chase had never found electric shock play erotic, but Stacey looked like she was having a grand time, so who was he to judge.

When he finally got to the corner where he was pretty sure Brighton and Ashley were, the low, mournful sound of someone in real pain reached his ears and set his teeth on edge. He stood rooted to the spot for a second, his mind at war with itself. Interrupting a scene was bad play etiquette, *unless* someone was in danger. But what was he really hearing? Was it even Ashley and Brighton?

As he debated, he heard the unmistakable sound of bamboo whipping through the air and making contact, followed again by that pained, ragged moan. The thought of Ashley, or anyone for that matter, broken to the level of suffering the cries implied spurred Chase into action. Aware he might not even be in the right spot, and that there was a chance he was going to make a total ass of himself, Chase pushed past the screened partition to see for himself what was going on.

The scene that met his eyes left him paralyzed again, but only for the split second it took his mind to process what he was seeing. Ashley was slumped forward against a railing, her wrists cuffed to it, her hands purple from lack of circulation. She was still in her waist cincher, but her skirt and shoes were off. The skin on her ass and thighs was heavily welted with a crisscross of dark red lines.

Brighton stood behind and just to the side of her, steadily flicking the cane against tortured flesh with a practiced hand.

Maybe for someone like Lotus Flower, who was trained to take it, and craved this level of intensity, the scene would have been appropriate. Maybe. For a novice like Ashley, Chase would have bet his very life the scene had gone way past consensual. Why hadn't she used her safeword?

These thoughts took only seconds to ripple through Chase's mind before rage exploded in his head like a crashing tsunami, sweeping away all rational thought in its wake. In two strides he was at Ashley's side, shoving Brighton violently out of his way.

He turned the keys in both cuffs and pulled them open. Ashley's hands fell limply to her sides and she slumped the rest of the way down, landing on her knees. Chase reached down, intending to lift her into his arms, but before he could, he was hauled up and thrown with considerable force against wall. He was stunned for a moment by the impact.

Leaping to his feet, he was ready when Brighton came at him, fists raised. He was desperately aware that Ashley needed him. At least she wasn't bleeding, but she clearly needed some aftercare. She needed someone to hold her in his arms and soothe her, someone to make sure she hadn't been harmed. Someone to explain that what had just happened to her wasn't, or shouldn't have been, part of the scene.

The last thing he wanted was a fist fight with this asshole, especially not while Ashley needed him. He ducked just as Brighton swung, and it went wide. He edged toward the girl, his eyes trained on his assailant.

Brighton swung again, and again Chase tried to dodge out of range, but this time he wasn't fast enough. Brighton's punch caught him on the side of the head, setting off a ringing in his left ear.

"Who the fuck do you think you are?" Brighton's tone was outraged. The raw fury might have given Chase pause, if he hadn't been so angry himself.

"What the hell, Brighton!" he snarled back. "You went way over the line this time. You're done. You have no place in the scene. You're dangerous."

"She wanted it, you jackass. She's a pain slut, same as the rest. She needs to learn to take what's coming to her. You have no right to interfere with a Master and his sub." Brighton lunged again and this time Chase raised his fist, taking way too much satisfaction as it sank into Brighton's solar plexus. Brighton grunted and doubled over, finally giving Chase a chance to turn to Ashley.

She had managed to pull herself upright and was reaching for the skirt still puddled on the ground. Her hair was wild over her face, and tears were streaming down her cheeks.

Chase's heart ached for her, beneath the seething rage reserved for Brighton. He tossed him a glance to make sure he wasn't up and ready for more action, but the man remained kneeling, clutching his gut and gasping for air.

Chase picked up the skirt and held it out for Ashley. She grabbed it and stepped into it, stumbling a little as she pulled it up, her eyes flickering constantly toward Brighton. Chase saw her fingers were trembling as she fumbled with her zipper. At least the circulation had returned to her hands, which were no longer purple from the too-tight cuffs. Who used police cuffs for a scene, lined or not? What the fuck was wrong with John Brighton?

Chase forced his tone into something approaching calm so as not to upset Ashley further. Gently he said, "Please, let me help you."

Mutely she turned her back to him, but dropped her shaking hands. "Thanks," she said in a tiny voice. Relief surged through him that she'd finally said something, anything. He examined her welted ass surreptitiously as he zipped her skirt. The welts were pretty severe and would leave marks for easily a week or more, but at least the prick hadn't broken the skin, and there shouldn't be any scarring.

When she was dressed again, her shoes on, Chase said, "Ashley. I'm so sorry this happened. It's not supposed to be like this, I promise you. He took advantage. He didn't pay attention to your body or what you needed. He betrayed your trust."

He tried to get her to look at him, but she kept her face averted, refusing to make eye contact. He could see that her cheeks were flushed and still stained with tears. Worried, he said, "Let me take you back to the motel. You need some aftercare, some down time to process all this. Okay?"

He reached for her arm, thinking how he'd fantasized so much over the last two days about being alone with her, but not like this. Not cleaning up the terrible mess another man had made.

She shrugged his hand away, shaking her head violently. "No," she said, her voice wavering. She took a breath and said with more force, "Leave me alone. Just leave me be. I can take care of myself. I don't want you or him." She shot a venomous look in Brighton's direction that would have made Chase whoop in triumph if she weren't also rejecting him in the process.

She moved toward the entrance, her gait unsteady but determined. "This whole thing was a mistake. I don't belong here. I never should have come."

"No," he tried, moving toward her, again reaching for her, unable to accept that she was going to leave without him. "You need someone right now. If not me, someone. Stacey, where is she? I'll get her."

But Ashley hadn't stayed to listen. She pushed past the still kneeling Brighton and disappeared beyond the screen. Chase started to follow her, but Brighton chose that moment to reach for Chase's ankle, jerking him off balance.

They began to tussle again, knocking a screen over in the process. Brighton was smashing his fists again and again into the side of Chase's head, but Chase barely felt the blows. Helpless fury over the turn of events had lent him a strength he wouldn't otherwise have had.

Chase was easily six inches shorter and forty pounds lighter than Brighton. Nevertheless he managed to knock the other man to the ground, straddling his chest and pinning him with his knees. He smashed his fist into Brighton's nose, taking furious pleasure as he heard the unmistakable snap of bone.

Suddenly the area was swarming with people, and both Chase and Brighton were hauled to their feet and pulled away from each other. Blood was gushing from Brighton's nose and Chase couldn't hear what was being said around him over the steady ringing in both ears.

Marty was waving his arms and yelling something, his face mottled with anger. Chase struggled against the strong grip of whoever was holding his arms pinned back. He craned back to see it was Jacob Presley, all three hundred something pounds, with plenty of solid muscle beneath the fat, intent on holding him still.

"Let me go," he said, his voice echoing in his head. "I need to find Ashley. It's urgent, damn it." Jacob loosened his grip enough for Chase to shrug him off.

"You two need to calm down," Marty was saying, and Chase was relieved to realize he could hear him now. The ringing had subsided for the most part, though his head was a box of pain and there was a knot the size of a small apple below his left ear.

Marty was mopping at Brighton's bloody nose with a large bandana. "I can't believe you guys. Here I expected to find some newbie idiot wannabes fighting over some girl, and I find out it's my two pros. What gives?"

"That bathtard," Brighton began, the righteous indignation clear in his tone, though his broken nose was affecting his ability to enunciate. "He broke my nothe. I'll thue, Saunders. I'll thue your butt!" Brighton began to babble about Chase attacking him and ruining his scene. Though a part of Chase knew he should stay and defend himself, he was too worried about Ashley to worry about himself at that moment.

"Sorry guys, I'd love to stay and chat, but there's a girl who might be really hurt, courtesy of dickwad over there." He pointed at Brighton, who glared at him.

Without waiting to hear Brighton's retort, Chase pushed his way through the gaping crowd that had gathered around them, desperately seeking the girl who'd fled the scene.

He moved quickly through the room, scanning it for any sign of her flying red hair, but she was nowhere to be seen. Though many folks had continued to scene, unaware of the fight that had taken place in the back, a small crowd of people surged toward him. He knew it was a matter of minutes before the news of the big fight rippled like wildfire through the place. Chase shrugged off the questions, intent on finding Ashley if he could.

His gut told him she was gone and he had a sinking feeling it was for good.

Chapter 7

It had started to rain, the droplets pelting against Kate's face and bare shoulders as she walked the two blocks from the warehouse to the motel. She hurried along, clutching her purse protectively to her side, anxious to get away from the dungeon and the people inside it.

Her ass and thighs still stung, but at least she wasn't bleeding. She'd reached back gingerly while pulling on her skirt, half-afraid when she looked that her fingers would be bloody. The hurt was less in her body and more in her spirit. Tears welled again as she unwillingly relived the last hour in her mind.

She'd trusted him. So much for safe, sane and consensual. How had he forgotten what should have been second nature to a so-called pro? And what was her part in all this? What was it about Master John that had blinded her reason? Usually she was so good at figuring out a person's character and discerning their true intentions.

Well, if she were honest, she had been aware he thought he was god's gift to sub girls, but she'd suspended her usual contempt for ego, blinded by his good looks and the whole adventure on which she'd embarked. She'd gone along, allowing Stacey and Master John to convince her, instead of following her initial impulse to refuse. She'd let his persuasive manner and his very handsome face disarm her. She'd been a fool.

Finally at the motel, Kate used her card key to gain access into the building. She waited impatiently for the elevator. When it finally came, she was forced to share it with two seedy-looking guys who kept staring at her. She hugged herself, keeping her eyes on the numbers until the elevator arrived at her floor.

She stepped out with relief and walked quickly to her room. Once inside, she leaned a moment against the locked door, careful not touch her tender bottom or thighs to the wood. She took several deep breaths. Her heart, which had pounded so hard toward the end of the caning that she'd very nearly passed out, still hadn't returned to its normal pace. She needed to calm down. It was over. She was safe. She would be fine—eventually.

She looked around the small room, for a moment wishing she'd taken Chase up on the offer of company— but the prospect had been too humiliating. He'd warned her in advance not to scene with Master John, even if he hadn't come right out and said so in so many words. But she had ignored him, confident she could handle whatever Master John meted out, never dreaming he'd betray her trust.

"I said my safeword," she murmured aloud, her voice cracking. "Why didn't he stop?"

Kate closed her eyes, refusing to succumb to more tears. She took another few deep breaths, shook back her wet hair and made a decision. She would leave tonight. She would leave now.

She noticed the room phone was blinking, indicating a message. No one knew she was there, so it must be for Stacey. Kate didn't like the idea of leaving without saying goodbye, but there was no way she was staying any longer than she had to. There were trains out of Grand Central back to the valley until at least one in the morning. She'd catch the next one to Beacon where her car was waiting. Though the event didn't officially wind down until brunch the next morning, as far as Kate was concerned the event was over — for good.

She grabbed her few items of clothing from the rickety bureau, and from the closet with the hangers that were permanently attached to the rod. She just wasn't cut out for this BDSM stuff. Yeah, it intrigued her, but this was twice now that things had gone horribly awry. She was better off sticking to fantasy. What had possessed her to think she needed to feel the stroke of the cane in order to write about it? That's what imagination was for, and she had plenty of that, too much, she'd often been told.

She made a quick tour of the bathroom, grabbing the toiletries that were hers, smiling slightly at the sight of Stacey's huge collection of makeup, most of it strewn over the small countertop beside the old-fashioned sink.

She returned to the bedroom, sweeping the room once more, again noticing the blinking red light. She decided to check the message, just in case. Stacey's smoky voice said, "Hey, Ash. Hope you had a great time tonight with the gorgeous Master John. I'm calling because I got lucky!" Stacey giggled and Kate could hear the low rumble of male voices behind her. "Look, I gotta go. Ben and Matt are taking me to this way cool underground club. I don't know when or even if," another giggle, "I'll be back to the room, so definitely don't wait up. Talk to you in the morning."

Kate found a notepad by the phone, though there was no pen. Rooting in her bag, she retrieved one and scribbled, "Something came up. Had to leave early. It was great meeting you. Take care, Kate." She realized she'd signed her real name, and started to crumple the page and start over, until she remembered she'd confided already to Stacey about her true identity. And who cared anyway? She'd never see any of these people again. This scene was most definitely not for her.

~*~

It was already after nine before Chase managed to haul himself out of bed the next morning. The knot below his ear had gone down some, but he could see from the bruising in the mirror that he was sporting the makings of two black eyes. "Yeah," he said, trying to smile at his reflection, "but you should see the other guy."

After Ashley had fled, Chase had tried and failed to find Stacey in the dungeon the night before. Someone had finally volunteered that they'd seen her leaving a while earlier with Ben and Matt, a gay couple who were both Doms.

Frustrated, Chase had appealed to Jacob Presley for Ashley's room number at the motel, but Presley said he didn't know. Not knowing what else to do, Chase had gone over to the motel and settled himself in the lobby, hoping maybe she'd show up eventually, if she wasn't there already, and if she was, maybe she'd come down for a soda or something.

Apparently he'd eventually dozed off while waiting, and was embarrassed to be awakened by the night clerk, who informed him there was a homeless shelter three blocks over, and he needed to move on. Chase had looked blearily at his watch. It was three in the morning. Ashley wasn't going to appear and he knew it.

Skipping the subway, he took a cab from Queens to Manhattan for the brunch, hoping against hope she'd be there, though he knew the odds were slim to none. He was glad to discover once he arrived that at least Brighton hadn't shown up either. Stacey finally appeared toward the end of the morning, still in the company of Matt and Ben. Chase hurried toward her.

Eyeing his face, Stacey said, "Jesus, Chase. What the hell happened to you?"

"Is she okay?" Chase burst out, ignoring the question.

"Is who okay?" Stacey looked blank.

"Ashley! Who else would I be talking about?" Chase frowned with impatience.

"Oh, why didn't you say so? She had to leave early. She left me a note. I didn't, uh, make it back to the motel until this morning." Stacey beamed at the two men standing beside her and turned back to Chase with a comical leer.

"Hey, Stace," one of the guys said. "We're going to grab some breakfast before it's all gone. Can we get you something?"

Stacey glanced at the couple. "No, that's okay. I'll get something in a minute. I want to talk to Chase." They wandered away. Chase felt his heart sink. Ashley was gone, as he'd feared. Stacey reached for his face, lightly touching his cheek. "I repeat the question. What the hell happened to you? You look like shit."

"Gee, thanks." Chase tried to grin but didn't quite manage it. "I got into a fight. With John Brighton."

"Master John! How come?" Stacey put her hand to her mouth. "Oh my god, it wasn't over Ashley, was it? Wow, two guys actually coming to blows over who gets the girl..."

"No, nothing like that. Brighton botched a scene — big time. He took her way past consensual. She was nearly unconscious when I first found them." Chase closed his eyes, trying to keep the rage still seething just below the surface from boiling over. "It's not the first time I've suspected he oversteps, but it's the first time I had definitive proof. He doesn't respect women. He's a bully in Dom's clothing."

Stacey's eyes wide. "Oh my god! Poor Ashley! I left early with the guys. I should have checked on her first. It never occurred to me...I can't believe it. And you guys had a knockdown, drag out fight? I bet M&M were livid."

"They weren't thrilled, but we didn't really fight until after Ashley had run away. By the time I extricated myself from the asshole, she was gone. That's why I need your help. I have to find her. I need to make sure she's okay."

Stacey nodded. "Well, she swore me to secrecy, but I agree with you. We should track her down. Ashley is her pen name. She's a romance author. Ashley Kendall. She used her pen name for the event. Her real name's Kate."

Chase took a moment to absorb this. It would take some mental adjustment to rethink her as Kate, though the name suited her better, he thought. "What's her last name? Kate what?"

Stacey pursed her lips and studied the ceiling, as if the name might be printed up there. She stroked her chin. "Hmmm," she said slowly. "I can't remember. Something with an A, I think. Anderson. Yeah. I think that was it. Kate Anderson. Or wait." Stacey wrinkled her nose in concentration. "Allen." She paused. "No, it was Anderson. I'm pretty sure."

She didn't sound very sure to Chase, but at least it was something to go on. "She's from Manhattan?" he asked.

"No. Somewhere upstate. Some valley. Hudson Valley. Yeah. That's it. But Chase," Stacey put her hand on his arm, her voice suddenly gentle. "Did it occur to you maybe she doesn't want to be found? She's a grown woman. She was obviously well enough to leave me a note, pack her stuff and skedaddle. Maybe it's best to leave well enough alone."

A part of him knew Stacey was right. Ashley, or rather Kate, hadn't asked Chase to intervene. Maybe he'd misread the whole scene, and she'd wanted what was happening to her. But every time he closed his eyes, he saw her face, the flushed cheeks with tears streaming down them, and the hurt and confusion palpable in her eyes.

No, he was sure it had gone way beyond consensual. He had to reach out to her. To explain it wasn't supposed to be like that. She'd been cheated by Master John. She'd been betrayed. He would find a way to connect with her. No matter what.

~*~

Normally Chase would have been long gone. He'd been paid for his time for the workshops, and there was no reason to stick around. The event had wrapped up after the brunch and some closing remarks by Marty and Marianne, which included an apology for the "ruckus" that had been inadvertently caused. Brighton was nowhere in evidence, and Chase didn't ask where he was, glad he didn't have to face the guy, afraid if he did, he might punch him again.

Power Play had only rented the warehouse space for the weekend. M&M kept the partition screens and larger BDSM equipment in a shed on their property in Westchester County. Most of the people still around were in the dungeon, packing up.

Only Jacob Presley remained upstairs, busily clacking on his laptop keyboard. Chase approached him. In what he hoped was a calm, rational voice, Chase asked Presley for Ashley Kendall's email address. "I just want to make sure she's okay after what Brighton pulled last night. She apparently split right after the scene."

Presley shook his head. "Sorry, Chase. No can do. Emails are proprietary." He executed a few clicks, hit return and then stared at his computer screen. "Ashley Kendall selected the 'do not share' tab for email or any other personal information on her registration form. If I go handing out her email address, I'm violating her privacy. It would compromise not only her integrity, but the integrity of Power Play. I'm sure you understand."

Chase bit his tongue to keep from saying something sarcastic about Power Play, which, while a worthy group, was really just a handful of kinky folk into public BDSM play. It wasn't like he was asking for her criminal record or classified CIA files or something. "If you'd seen her, Jake," he tried one more time. "Brighton abused her. She was terrified. She ran off. I just want to make sure she's okay."

Presley shook his head again, crossing his beefy arms over his chest for emphasis. "I get what you're saying, but it ain't happening. No offense, but I don't think she asked you to be her knight in shining armor, did she? If she wants to be in touch, she can email me. If she does, I'll definitely let you know. How's that?"

That sucks, Chase wanted to say. "Okay, thanks," he said instead. "Guess I'm going to head back to Queens."

"Okay. Sorry I couldn't help you, buddy," Presley said. "And listen, try to stay out of trouble, okay? We don't like our pros beating on each other. Isn't good for our reputation."

"It's not good for your reputation to employ a guy who doesn't respect limits. John Brighton is dangerous."

Presley peered at Chase. "With all due respect, we've been involved with John Brighton for over five years. Yeah, there's been the occasional complaint that he's intense, but that's one of the reasons he's such a big draw. The women are literally lining up to scene with that dude. Now, while your bondage workshops are well received..." Presley trailed off, but Chase knew where he was going with it. Naturally somewhat of a loner anyway, Chase's rope making and bondage gear business was handled almost entirely online, and he spent most of his waking hours holed up in his workshop. He'd only reentered the pubic scene within the last few months, as a way to try and force himself back into the world.

Presley continued. "You know people come and go at these events. No one's taking attendance. She's paid in full. I don't care if she decides to skip the brunch.

Look, nobody saw this so-called 'abuse' except for you. She managed to get out of there on her own volition, so it couldn't have been that bad, no matter what you thought you saw. As far as Master John's concerned, without any complaint from the girl, it comes down to a case of you said, he said. Just so you're prepared, you should know he's already lodged a complaint with M&M about you. I don't know what they're planning on doing about it at this point, but I'd watch my step if I were you."

Chase was too stunned to respond. He pressed his lips together, bouncing lightly on the balls of his feet, his muscles tensing like they were preparing for another fight. Aware he had to contain his anger, Chase stood tall, ramming his hands into his pockets to keep them from curling into fists.

Focus, he reminded himself. *This is about Ashley — about Kate. Nothing else matters right now.* Without another word, he walked away. Presley resumed tapping at his keyboard.

But Chase didn't leave the building. He found a spot against a wall near the lockers, out of Presley's line of vision. He was a patient man, he reminded himself, but also a determined one.

From time to time he leaned forward until he could see Presley. The hulking man was still bent over his laptop. From his corner, Chase surreptitiously watched Presley, waiting for his chance. Stacey and Presley were probably right. Kate didn't want or require saving. He should let it alone. He should walk out and head home, and put this whole sorry business behind him.

He'd nearly convinced himself to do just that, but Presley chose that moment to stand up and amble away, leaving his laptop behind on the card table. Chase remained where he was, watching until Presley disappeared down the stairs.

Cautiously Chase moved out from behind the lockers. No one else was in sight. He could hear them talking and moving things below. He seized his chance, moving quickly toward the laptop.

He scanned its desktop and saw a file that read *PP Registration*. He opened it. Inside were documents titled by date. He found that weekend and clicked again. There they were—all the attendees with pertinent information such as how they had paid for the event, their D/s orientation and, yes, their email address. Some had included a phone number, but hers was not filled in. There was no snail mail address, but email was better than nothing.

When he read the address he gave a small grunt. It was ridiculously obvious, once he saw it. Ashley@AshleyKendall.com. Made sense. She was an author, according to Stacey. She probably had a website, and that was the email address associated with it. She probably had a blog and a Facebook account and Twitter too, all of it as Ashley, Kate safely incognito.

Kate Anderson. It was a pretty common name. If it was even the right name. Stacey had been rather vague.

Might be Allen or maybe she'd got it wrong altogether. At least he had the pen name, and now an email address. He'd write to her, and who knew, maybe he'd get lucky and she'd write back.

"And if she doesn't, Saunders," he said to himself, "then you need to let it, and her go."

Chapter 8

Though she'd only been gone from home a few days, she felt like she'd returned from the wars, wounds and all. It was good to be back in her safe, sleepy village. Horses on a nearby farm were grazing outside her window, their coats shiny in the summer sunlight.

She stared at them, willing the sense of peace watching them usually brought her, but it didn't come. By the time she'd finally made it all the way home it was nearly three in the morning. She'd gone straight to bed and somehow managed to sleep, though she'd awakened by seven, the sound of a woodpecker as insistent as a jackhammer outside her window.

She gasped when she saw her bottom in the mirror that morning. It was covered with welts, some pink, some red, some nearly purple. Her thighs were similarly marked. They didn't really hurt that much anymore, but she wondered if they'd leave scars. The thought was very unsettling. How had she been so stupid as to hook up with that man? Why was he allowed to do what he did? Should she tell someone? Maybe email Master Presley and let him know what had happened?

The thought was too embarrassing, at least for the moment. Maybe in a day or a week, when her emotions had calmed down, when her flesh had healed. And anyway, Chase Saunders had probably told them. He seemed like a very responsible type.

She'd been so blinded by Master John's charismatic attraction, his masterful attitude, that she hadn't really focused much on Chase. She had sensed his dominance during the workshop, but it was a more subdued kind of behavior. She found herself wondering how that might change one on one, when Chase was not the instructor, but the lover.

Chase's words came back to her. *It's not supposed to be like this. He took advantage. He betrayed your trust.* Chase had saved her from a man who had gone past the boundaries of safe and consensual. It was humiliating that Chase had been witness to it, since he was the one who'd warned her against John in the first place.

Kate tried to go about her normal routine, making coffee, settling down at her computer to check email and any royalty statements that might have arrived, checking her Facebook and blog for reader comments.

She opened her latest manuscript, the BDSM novel she was supposed to be writing, the one this trip was supposed to give her inspiration for. She stared at the screen, her fingers limp, her mind empty.

She was restless and agitated. She was angry and confused. She wanted to talk to someone about what had happened, but who?

She thought of Stacey, but rejected the idea. Not only did she not know how to contact her, but she found herself actually resenting Stacey in a way. After all, she was the one who practically forced Kate into the scene with Master John.

No, that wasn't fair and she knew it. Kate was a big girl, and she was the one who had made the decision. She'd gone with the flashy guy, excited not only by the idea of being with him, but pleased by the ego stroke of his choosing her.

With a sigh, she closed the document and started to rise from her desk, but the pinging sound that indicated the arrival of a new email caught her attention and she sat back down.

She didn't recognize the email address, but she got fan mail several times a week, which she always answered immediately. She began to read.

Dear Ashley,

I hope it's okay to contact you. Stacey clued me in on your writing career, and I looked up your website. Please forgive me if you consider this email a violation of your privacy, but after what happened last night and the way you disappeared afterwards I was and am very concerned that you are okay. I interrupted your scene last night because what I heard and saw made me concerned for your safety and well being.

Shit. I'm laughing at myself right now, because I just spent nearly thirty minutes composing and recomposing that one paragraph, while trying to figure out how to express my concern without pushing myself into where I may not be wanted.

When you ran out of the warehouse it was clear, as it should have been to anyone, you were very upset after what you experienced. I am reaching out to you because I really want to know that you are okay and if you aren't, to help you in any way I can. I know we barely know each other, but please understand that I am here for you … to talk, to listen, to be a friend. Email me or better yet, call me any time, day or night. I mean it Ashley, any time, day or night.

I know you are new to the scene and I hope you will understand that what happened to you has nothing to do with what BDSM is really about. The romance and pleasure of a consensual exchange of power was lost in the abuse you were subjected to. It is understandable if you decided never to have anything to do with BDSM, but I also know something in your heart brought you to the event. You wouldn't have been there if you didn't feel that "something" is out there waiting for you.

Ashley, the tears I saw on your face and the betrayal I know you felt are indelibly etched in my mind. If you need a friend, someone to talk to, I'm here.

Chase Saunders

His cell phone number was listed below. Kate wiped away a tear she hadn't known had slipped over one cheek. What a kind man to write such a thing. She thought about his words, that what happened with Master John had nothing to do with BDSM. And yet…and yet when they'd started the scene, she'd been incredibly aroused by being bound and at his mercy. She'd remained aroused in spite of the caning. No, *because* of it. But he had gone too far. He had slashed through the tenuous bonds of a fledgling trust and now

Kate wasn't sure she'd ever have the courage to try again.

She was tempted to push the whole thing out of her mind, the same way she'd pushed Victor's rejection of her and her submissive impulses under wraps these past few years. She would go on with her tidy, quiet life, pretending she was fine, letting the welts fade away along with the memories.

And yet she knew she couldn't do that. Not this time. Even if she managed to put it out of her mind from day to day, the psychic wound of the event would lay buried deep in her heart like a trapped bit of broken glass, covered eventually by scar tissue, but never fully removed.

Chase's email had unlocked something in her. She wasn't going to shove it down, she realized. Not this time.

She hit the reply button.

Dear Chase,

Thanks for the email.

She paused, wondering what to say. Did she confide her true feelings to this man? And if so, how much? A sudden ache to connect—to tell someone, anyone, how she was feeling assailed her. Her fingers began to move over the keyboard, almost of their own accord.

Thanks for not rubbing it in with an "I told you so." The stupid thing is, I thought I could handle it. I thought I knew what I was doing, getting involved with a guy who talked half the time like he was reading a script from some cheesy porno flick.

He also told me a little fear was a good thing. That should have been my next clue.

Remember you said I could always use my safeword? That that would stop the action cold? I did use it, when I could finally get my head around what was going on enough to form the word. Either he didn't hear it, or he ignored it. That was when I realized I was hanging out there over the abyss, with no safety net. I think that's when I really lost it.

Thing is, I've always wanted to experience the power, what did you call it? The romance of a consensual exchange of power. I wanted to understand what that really means, on a gut level. I wanted to write about it. I wanted to create characters who speak directly to the reader. Characters who live and breathe and bleed and break our hearts and power our dreams...

I thought, idiot that I am, that some stupid scene at a BDSM play party would give me the tools I needed to tell a BDSM story that resonated, that mattered. How naïve is that? You mentioned I'm new to the scene, but that's not entirely true. A few years back me and my then significant other did some experimenting. He wasn't a true Dom, but he was willing and eager, at first anyway, to try. Neither of us really knew what we were doing, but there were a few times when it clicked. When something inside me said, "Yes, that's it. That's who I am. This is where I belong."

It's almost like it was a physical space I would inhabit, though only for moments a time. A space where I felt right, complete somehow for once. I even felt that with Master John at first. When I was cuffed and exposed, waiting for that first stroke of the cane — it went beyond sexual excitement, or anticipation of the unknown. There was a certain, I don't know, rightness about it. Like I had been waiting all my life for this, and had found it at last.

That's what makes it so hard, you see. First with Victor, then with Master John, I gave my trust, and it was abused. I have to conclude I'm the one at fault. What's that old adage, "Fool me once, shame on you. Fool me twice, shame on me."

I should have seen the signs. I should have followed my gut instead of, uh, other organs. I should have listened to you. You tried to warn me, but I thought I knew better. Don't waste your time, Chase. I'm fine, or I will be. I've decided BDSM is not for me, except as a passing dream of what might have been.

Kate stopped, barely aware of what she had written. It had poured out of her in whole sentences, composed behind the scenes of conscious thought, coming faster than her fingers could type.

She scrolled back up and read her words.

When she was done, she shook her head and sighed. What was she thinking? Too much information. Chase Saunders didn't want to know this shit about her. He had been freaked out by her tears, was all. Most men couldn't handle a woman's tears, no matter the circumstance.

She highlighted what she'd written and hit the delete button.

She started over, her fingers moving slowly, her heart heavy.

Dear Chase,

Thanks for the email. I appreciate your concern. I am doing okay. A little shook up, but nothing time won't heal. I don't really think contacting you further is what I need right now. I'd like a little distance from the whole thing.

Take care and thanks again,

Ashley Kendall

~*~

Kate settled down the next morning at her desk with a cup of coffee, which she sipped while waiting for the computer to boot up. She opened her email, scrolling through the new messages, deleting the junk and moving the few that required action into a special folder.

Her eye dropped back to Chase's email. She reread his heartfelt words and half regretted the terse reply she'd sent, wondering what he must think of her. Noticing the website address in the signature, she clicked on it — *SensualRopeArt.com.*

The tag line at the top of the page read, *Bondage gear and handmade rope for every taste and level, from the not-so vanilla to the hard core enthusiast. Enter here to explore your fantasies and realize your dreams.*

There were several tabs, including products, testimonials, frequently asked questions and videos. Intrigued, Kate clicked on the video tab, which took her to a selection of how-to videos. There were videos on the basic two column tie and single limb cuff she'd learned at his workshop, and instructions on more complex bondage like the chest harness, hog tie, hair tie and full body harness.

Chase was featured in the videos, along with a thin, blonde woman who served as his subject. They were wearing matching black T-shirts with the RopeArt logo. Chase's hair was longer in the videos, curling down his neck. He was actually a pretty good looking guy, she realized, now that she wasn't being blinded by Master John's blond perfection and provocative manner.

The videos were informative and practical, not sensual per se. Chase offered the same easy, pleasant interaction with the camera as he had at the workshop. He talked to the viewer as if to a friend, without a trace of ego or self-consciousness. He exuded a certain quiet, sexy calm that was so different from the smoldering fire just beneath the surface that Kate had experienced with Master John. Chase was clearly in his element as he demonstrated quick but elegant and effective bondage techniques on his very willing subject, binding her in any number of sensual positions.

The last video on the page was titled *Suspension Bondage*. The model in this one was a different woman. She wasn't wearing the black uniform T-shirt, but rather a red silk dress that hugged a slender but shapely frame. She was petite, coming barely to Chase's shoulder, with long dark hair flowing down her back.

Chase demonstrated how to safely suspend someone with stainless steel suspension rings. The crimson rope he used matched the girl's dress and offset her luxurious long black hair. The act of binding the girl was erotic in itself, coils of soft, strong rope wound around wrists and thighs, looped in a figure eight over breasts and hips.

Kate wasn't really paying attention to his explanations or demonstration. She was watching his face, his expression when he looked at the girl, and hers when she looked at him.

"They're lovers," she whispered aloud, not sure how this made her feel. She realized she'd just assumed Chase was not involved with anyone. He'd said to call any time, day or night. Would he have done that with the beautiful woman in the video sleeping beside him?

Or was theirs a Master/slave relationship where he kept her in chains at the foot of the bed, his possession with no say in whom he talked to when? Kate shook her head. She just didn't see Chase as that kind of Dom. What had he written?

The romance and pleasure of a consensual exchange of power.

Did Master John even understand the concept, the possibility that romance could be involved? Kate snorted. He was no kind of Dom, she understood that now. Chase had called him a bully and that's just what he was.

She watched the suspension demo video again, certain she was right about the pair. Those two were or had been at the time of the video, lovers. Did he suspend her like that in the privacy of their bedroom, naked and bound for his pleasure? What would it be like to feel those ropes tight around wrists, chest, thighs and ankles, unable to move or resist?

All at once, Master John's handsome face insinuated itself into her mind's eye, his smile cruel, the cane clutched in his hands. With a shudder, Kate closed her browser and left the computer. What she needed was another cup of coffee.

No. What she needed was some fresh air and a good long run. She would listen to music on her MP3 player and jog along the country roads. She would let the physical exertion of the run take over, taxing her muscles, emptying her mind and easing her spirit.

~*~

Kate couldn't breathe. The hand over her mouth was suffocating her. Hard, boney fingers were pressing into her cheek. In a panic, she jerked against her restraints and cried out from the pain. Her wrists were bound to a wooden bar with barbed wire that cut into her skin. The blood was dripping steadily, two red pools on the concrete floor.

She was naked in a room full of mirrors. She could see him behind her, a blond god, but something was wrong with his eyes. They were red and filled with hate. He took his hand away from her mouth and she gasped for breath.

"So I can hear you scream," he said, his voice low, filling her with dread.

The cane sliced against her bare back. In the mirror behind her she saw the cut, a long, angry red line, and she felt the ooze of warm blood sliding over her skin.

"Red," she tried to scream, but nothing came, no sound. There was only her own reflection, her mouth open in an O of mute agony.

"You're a pain slut, just like all of them. You need the pain. You beg and plead for me to stop, but you know you want it. Deal with it. Embrace it. I'm not going to stop until *I* decide you've had enough."

He pulled her head back by the hair, but it was no longer her hair. It was fire, fire licking against her scalp, scalding her cheeks, burning her flesh. Again she tried to scream, but her voice was silent in the void of her own terror. He loomed behind her, his face like a demon, twisted with menace as he raised the cane again.

She awoke suddenly, gasping and crying, her body drenched in a cold sweat. Her heart felt like it was thudding out of her chest, banging so hard it felt bruised against the bone. She reached for the bedside lamp, her hand shaking so badly it took several tries to turn the switch.

"Only a dream. Only a dream," she said aloud. Her mouth was dry and she reached for the glass of water she kept by her bed at night, but her trembling fingers ended up knocking it to the floor.

She yanked off a pillowcase and dropped it over the spill. She swung her feet over the side of the bed and went into the bathroom, where she splashed water on her face and neck. She cupped her hands and drank several mouthfuls of water. Peeling off her sweat-soaked nightgown, she dropped it to the floor.

She stepped into the shower and turned it on. "Only a dream," she repeated. "A nightmare. Let it go. Forget it. Think about nice things." She closed her eyes, letting the warm spray wash away the nightmarish images still slithering in her head.

But it didn't work. Even while she tried to imagine the horses out at pasture and the calm of an ocean's waves flowing and ebbing, it was the *feeling* of the nightmare that lingered. It hung over her like a damp mist, like a shroud, a finger of dread still dragging its way up and down her spine. She knew she wouldn't be able to go back to sleep.

She climbed out of the shower, dried and put on a fresh nightgown and panties. Wrapping her hair in a towel, she went into the kitchen, poured herself a glass of orange juice and went into her study. She sat at her laptop, thinking to distract herself with some mundane task, but found herself opening her email account.

There was nothing new from Chase Saunders, not that she expected it after her reply. She found herself oddly disappointed. After spending nearly an hour watching him on his website, she felt closer to him, as if they were friends. Could she get past the humiliation of his witnessing her botched scene with Master John?

There was a cry outside the window and Kate gave a little involuntary gasp, her blood running cold. She hugged herself, and tried to laugh off her anxiety when she realized she'd only heard an owl hooting in the distance. Yet the terror of the dream still lingered. She need to make contact with another human being to wrest herself from the clammy grip of the nightmare.

She realized she wanted to call Chase Saunders. She wanted to hear his calming voice and his peaceful, easy tone soothe her. She looked at the time in the lower right corner of her screen: 3:16 a.m. She'd certainly be waking him up if she called.

She was being silly anyway—it was just a bad dream. It would fade in time, especially if she focused on something else. She would watch TV or read a book. She didn't need to call anyone, not at three in the morning, for heaven's sake. She was a grown woman, not a child afraid of monsters under the bed.

She got up from the computer and went back into the kitchen. Opening the cabinet where she kept her wine, she reached behind the bottles, pulling out the bottle of Scotch someone had given her as a gift the Christmas before.

She opened it, aware her hands were still shaking, and poured herself a stiff drink, which she downed neat. It made her eyes water and her throat burn, but she felt like she needed it. She poured herself a second one, adding some ice this time, and carried it with her back to the study, back to her computer, where she stared at Chase's phone number for another minute or two, silently arguing with herself.

She picked up her cell phone from the desk and punched in the number. She stared at it, unable to find the nerve to complete the call. What if the lovely girl in the red dress was asleep beside him, curled into his arms? Who the hell was Kate to disturb the sleeping couple?

Maybe she could call her friend Jean instead. Jean was a night owl. She might even still be up. But what would Kate say? I had this horrible nightmare about this guy called Master John that I met in a BDSM dungeon?

None of her friends knew about her experiments with Victor, or her secret and long-held submissive fantasies. If she was going to confide in any of them, Jean was the one, but not at three in the morning, and not in the frame of mind she was in. Jean would think she'd lost her mind.

Maybe she had?

She downed the rest of the second drink.

He'd said to call any time. If he hadn't meant it, he shouldn't have said it. Anyway, odds were good he wouldn't pick up at that hour anyway, and the call would go directly to voicemail. If it did, she'd just hang up.

She pushed send and held her breath while the call connected.

It rang several times before she heard the sleepy, low rumble of a man's voice.

"Hello?"

Kate's heart squeezed in her chest.

"Hello?" Chase asked again, more clearly this time.

"Hi. It's Ashley Kendall."

Chapter 9

The alarm was buzzing, which was strange. Since Chase had quit his job as a systems analyst two years before, he'd stopped setting the alarm. He reached out, fumbling in the dark for the snooze button, but when he pushed it the sound continued.

He finally came awake enough to realize it wasn't his alarm, but his cell phone that was ringing. He glanced at the clock—3:34 a.m.—praying his dad hadn't had another heart attack.

He squinted at the screen, not recognizing the phone number. "Hello?" There was silence. He waited a beat and said again, "Hello?"

"Hi. It's Ashley Kendall."

Ashley!

"Hey." He came instantly and fully awake, unable to stop the broad smile that spread over his face. After her email basically blowing him off, he honestly hadn't expected to hear from her again.

Then he realized she was calling in the middle of the night—probably not the best sign. "Everything okay?"

"Um." She gave a small, nervous laugh. "I'm really sorry to bother you like this. It's crazy, I know, but you said—"

"I said call any time, and I meant it. I'm glad you did. What's got up you at this hour?"

"I feel kind of silly but, well. I had this...nightmare. I can't seem to shake it. I'm afraid if I go back to sleep I'll have it again."

"Was the nightmare about what happened?"

"Yeah." Her voice dropped to a whisper.

"I'm sorry," Chase said, and he meant it. He could feel the anger rising again. He wanted to smash Brighton's pretty boy face in. He forced himself to get a grip. Ashley didn't need a testosterone-fueled rant right now, she needed his ear.

"It's good you called. Talk to me. Sometimes saying it out loud takes away the sting of a bad dream. Puts it into perspective."

There was a pause at the other end of the line for so long Chase thought they might have lost the connection. "You still there?"

"Yes. I'm here. It was just so...horrible. He had me in this room full of mirrors. My wrists were bound with barbed wire, which was cutting deep into the skin. I was bleeding. I was screaming but there was no sound. He was like a devil, with these creepy red eyes...oh!" She made a little sobbing sound.

"Listen to me. It was just a dream. It's not real. You can let it go now. It's over." Chase felt his heart seize with compassion. If he'd been beside her, he would have taken her into his arms and stroked her hair, soothing her back to sleep.

But she didn't need his sympathy right now. She needed someone stable and calm to work her through her fear. "You okay?"

"Yes," she answered, her voice small.

I want you to listen to me. I know how real nightmares can feel. But they're not. They're just a way for your subconscious to process negative feelings. A way of purging the memory, of letting it go. Look, don't let that prick live rent-free in your head any longer. He's just not worth it.

"As far as we're concerned, from this moment forward, that guy, we won't even bother to say his name, doesn't exist. He's a bad dream, a lost cause. He's a loser who had a beautiful woman offer him the thing most precious in this world — her submission — and he betrayed that. He deserves to be consigned to nightmares, and then forgotten."

To his delight, she laughed, this time without apology. "You should be a therapist or something. I like that about living rent-free in my head. You're so right. I don't want to waste another second thinking about that guy."

"What guy?" Chase teased, and, to his delight, she laughed again.

"Okay, I get it. Thanks, Chase. I'm feeling better now. I'm sorry I bothered you in the middle of night. I feel like such a kid."

"Not at all. If you *hadn't* called, then I'd be mad." He didn't say his next thought, which was, after that email she'd sent back, he'd tried to reconcile himself to the fact he'd probably never hear from her again. He didn't admit he was secretly and selfishly glad she'd had that nightmare, if that's what it took to make her reach out to him.

Kate laughed again. Chase wished he could see her. He imagined her sitting up in her bed, as he was doing, her thick, shiny red hair falling in luscious waves to her shoulders, her breasts bare, the nipples rosy at their centers. He felt his cock rise and warned himself to cut it out. Though he was very glad she'd called, he didn't want to fool himself that there was more to it than there was. She'd called because she'd been spooked by a bad dream, and he had been handy. No point in making more out of it than that.

He didn't want her to hang up, not yet. To keep the conversation going, he said, "I visited your website. I'm quite impressed with all those novels you've written. You're the real thing, a bona fide author. I'm in awe."

"Oh stop. I write romance. I love doing it, but it's not great literature. I just enjoy telling a good love story. I love making up a world and inhabiting it with characters who sometimes come to mean more to me than real people. I sort of stumbled into publishing when a friend sent part of one of my manuscripts to a pretty well known New York publishing house and they called me, out of the blue, to ask for the rest of it."

"Wow, that's a great story. I got into rope making as a hobby too. I couldn't find good bondage rope that I liked so I did some research on how to make it myself. I never planned on its turning into a business."

"I was at your website too," she said, a shyness creeping into her tone.

"You were, huh? What did you think?"

"Very impressive. I learned a lot from watching the videos. You're a very good teacher."

"Thanks." Chase felt a happy warmth move through him at her praise, surprised how much it mattered from someone he barely knew. His site had won awards in the BDSM community, and he was starting to earn serious money with his products and seminars, but none of it seemed as sweet at that moment as her praise.

"There was one…" She paused.

He waited but when she didn't continue, prompted, "Yes? You had a question?"

"Um, no. No, never mind. It's not important." She yawned, adding, "I guess I should tell you my real name. Ashley Kendall is my pen name. I'm Kate. Kate Alexander."

For some reason this knowledge greatly pleased Chase. He smiled into the phone. "Nice to meet you, Kate. That name suits you. It's a lovely name."

"Thank you. I like the name Chase, too. It's unusual."

"Yeah." Chase didn't mention that his middle name was Newton. He had no idea what his parents had been thinking. Instead he said, "Do you think you can sleep now?"

Kate answered by yawning again loudly into the receiver. Chase laughed, and found himself yawning too. "I hope we talk again soon, Kate," he added, meaning it.

"Me too," she said softly. They said their goodnights and hung up, but Chase knew he, for one, would not be able to fall back asleep. He was…what *was* this feeling bouncing around inside him like a whole roomful of helium balloons? It had been so long since he'd felt it, he was almost unable to define it.

He was happy.

Chase followed up their phone conversation with a brief email the next morning, keeping it light and easy, with no reference to the negatives of their phone call. Kate replied with a similar breezy response. Her last line caught his attention. *I live about seventy miles from the city, up near Newburgh, but I do get down there from time to time to see my editor. Maybe next time I come down you can give me a tour of your rope making business.*

He interpreted the email any number of ways, first taking it solely on its face—she wanted to see how bondage rope was made—and running the gamut in his head until he concluded that she was subtly asking to scene with him. He emailed back that he would love to give her the full tour, wondering with an inward grin if she'd do a similarly obsessive teenage analysis of his words.

When he didn't hear back right away, he laughed at himself, reminding himself of his own best advice, which was not to push the river. Go with the flow and let things take their course. Kate was the first woman since Lisa who had so occupied his thoughts. He decided to savor this reawakening of emotions and let things move at their own pace. If nothing came of it, at least he knew he hadn't lost the capacity to feel.

Two days later Chase actually found a legitimate reason to call. He'd checked out Newburgh on the map and realized it wasn't that far from Kingston, which was where the guy who provided him with untreated hemp rope for his business lived. He was running low on the raw material, and while technically he didn't need to drive all the way up there to get it, he'd been meaning to meet the guy face to face for a while now, and this seemed as good a time as any.

Grinning at himself and feeling more like fifteen than thirty-five, Chase called Kate, who picked up after the second ring. "Hello?"

"Kate. It's Chase Saunders."

"Oh, hi." There was a smile in her voice that made him smile back.

They exchanged the usual pleasantries and then he got to the point. "Listen, I'm making a trip up to Kingston soon to pick up some supplies. That's not far from Newburgh, right? I was thinking, if you had the time, I'd love to take you to lunch." He realized he was holding his breath and chuckled to himself. *Don't push the river.*

"I would enjoy that," she replied. "I pretty much keep my own schedule. What day were you thinking?"

"I can't get away today or tomorrow, but I was thinking Friday? You pick the place and the time, and I'll be there."

~*~

Kate sipped her iced tea, her eyes on the door of Maude's Country Cooking, the small, quaint café where they'd agreed to meet. After spending quite a bit of time on Chase's website, she'd found herself speculating endlessly about his private life, and wondered why she hadn't just come out and ask. Maybe she would today. After all, he was driving all the way up from the city to see her.

Well, not specifically to see her, she reminded herself, since he had business in the area. Maybe she was just an afterthought. His good deed to check up on the traumatized sub girl who had called him in the middle of the night.

She thought again of the woman in red, at the way she'd looked at Chase with something approaching adoration while he bound her in red rope for the camera. What had happened after the camera was turned off, with her bound and offered like a ripe apple in an Eden of his making?

If the timing seemed right, maybe today she would ask, throwing out the question in a casual way. *That girl in the video...is she...are the two of you...?*

The door opened and Chase appeared, more handsome than she'd remembered him. He was wearing a white button-down shirt, untucked over blue jeans, though instead of the sneakers he'd had on at the weekend, he wore a pair of black square-toed boots. He had a small canvas bag slung over his shoulder.

He glanced around the room, his face lighting into a radiant smile when he saw her. She found herself smiling broadly back. She liked the deep dimples in either cheek and the laugh lines that crinkled at the corners of his eyes and bracketed his mouth.

She stood as he approached and he leaned forward, lightly kissing her cheek. "It's great to see you again, Ash — er, Kate." He smiled.

They sat down opposite one another at the small table. "Well, Ashley was the clueless one who didn't heed your advice."

"Kate." Chase reached across the small table and put his hand over hers. "You weren't clueless. You aren't to blame for what he did." His expression was kind, his voice gentle. "Tell me," he said softly, "did you use your safeword?"

Kate felt tears building behind her eyes and she blinked them back. "Yes. Though not soon enough. I think I was so shocked by what was happening that my brain sort of shut down."

Kate could actually see the fury flicker over Chase's face. She watched as he fought it, his expression easing back into calm. She wasn't used to someone caring so intensely about what happened to her, but instead of making her nervous, she realized it made her feel good.

"He had no right, Kate. You deserve so much better."

The waitress appeared a moment later, her pad at the ready. "Can I get you something to drink while you look at the menu? The peach iced tea is homemade. Made it myself."

Chase looked up at the heavyset woman. Her cheeks were flushed, wisps of blond hair escaping from a tight ponytail. She looked tired. Chase smiled. "That sounds perfect. Just what I need on a hot day like today. Thanks." The waitress beamed back at him and hurried away.

Chase turned back to Kate. "This seems like a nice place. I'm glad you suggested it. I never know where to grab a bite when I come up here."

"I was just here once, with a friend. But the food was fresh. They make good salads and sandwiches. Nothing fancy, but the apple streusel with vanilla ice cream is pure perfection."

Chase laughed. "A sweet tooth, huh?"

"My one weakness."

"Well, if you only have one, you're way ahead of the game."

The waitress returned with Chase's tea and took their orders. When she had gone, Chase said, "I brought you a present." Reaching into the canvas bag that he'd hung over the back of his chair, he pulled out a small coil of thick braided rope. What kind of present was *that*? He glanced at the face she must have been making and grinned. "No, that's not your present. That's a sample of the untreated hemp rope I get from my supplier. Touch it."

She did. It was rough and scratchy, the color of straw. Chase withdrew a second coil of rope, this one dyed a rich, inky black. "*This* is your present. A sample of my work. I thought you might like to see how I turn that," he pointed toward the hemp, "into this." He uncoiled a length and held it out to her.

"Give me your hand," he said softly.

She stared at the rope and swallowed, something shifting inside her, almost as if he'd reached in and pushed a secret button. She could feel a pulse throbbing in her throat and her nipples were suddenly erect. She found herself holding out both hands, the wrists touching.

Chase tilted his head and stared into her eyes, a half smile forming on his lips. Gently he took one of her hands, turning it palm up. He set the coil into it and sat back, a bemused expression on his face.

Kate found herself blushing. What had come over her? Holding out her wrists, as if he planned on binding her right there in at a café, for all the world to see. What had she been thinking?

She was grateful when he said nothing, certain he'd understood her gesture for precisely what it had been. Embarrassed, she was glad to have something to focus on. She uncoiled the rope, exclaiming, "It's so soft! I can't believe this was made from that rough stuff."

"We boil the hemp in industrial size pots in my garage and hand condition every piece until it's soft as silk, but much stronger. It doesn't wear and fray the way commercial rope does, and I have found some excellent dyes that make my rope not only functional, but beautiful."

"We?" *The girl in red...?*

"Yeah. I used to do it all alone, but I've had to hire help. I employ two other people and still we can barely keep up with the orders. Right now the work is done in my garage, but we've definitely outgrown it. I'm going to have to break down soon and find a space to rent."

"I'd love to see where you work," Kate said. "And where you shot those videos," she added, before she had a chance to censor herself.

"The videos...?" He cocked his head.

"On your website. You know, the how-to videos." The waitress brought their sandwiches and topped off their tea, putting her hand lightly on Chase's shoulder as she asked if she could get them anything else. He assured her they were fine, again meeting her eye with a pleasant smile. Kate liked that about him. She'd been a waitress while in college, and knew what a hard gig it was. Being treated like an equal fellow human being went a long way, she well knew.

He turned back to Kate once the waitress had gone. "Ah yes. I need to make some new ones. Those are all pretty old. We rented a studio for two days and did most of them on the first take. Marcy's great to work with."

"Marcy..." Kate echoed. *Here it comes,* she thought, *now he'll tell me about the beautiful model in the video, his partner in both work and play...*

"Yeah, she's very patient. She and her partner, Seth, work with me. She's actually the Domme in the relationship, but since Seth's six-foot-four, we decided she'd make the better model for the videos."

"She's the blonde, then." Kate realized she'd forgotten to breathe while he'd been speaking. What was the matter with her? Why did she care so much?

Chase looked slightly puzzled. "Yeah. Last I checked. The one in the videos."

"There was another woman." Kate felt an odd tightening in her stomach, sort of like when she'd been a child, standing out on the edge of the diving board at the town swimming pool, screwing up her courage to dive.

"Another woman?" Chase furrowed his brows.

"The suspension video. The girl in red."

The oddest thing happened then. Chase's eyes widened and a flush crept up his cheeks, only to fade so quickly he looked positively pale beneath the few days' sexy stubble.

"Are you okay?" Kate asked, suddenly concerned.

"I...I forgot that video was still on the site. I had meant...to remove it." He spoke haltingly, his voice subdued. He swallowed hard and stared down at the table.

"Chase. What's the matter? You look like you've seen a ghost."

He looked up again quickly, forcing a smile, though the pain remained ripe in his eyes. "I'm sorry. It's nothing."

"Is it that video with the girl in red? Is that what's upsetting you?"

Chase nodded. "Yeah."

Kate waited, but he added nothing more. He picked up his sandwich and began to eat. Kate sensed he wouldn't welcome additional questions right then. Clearly she'd touched on a very sensitive topic. Had they had a bad breakup? She guessed that's probably what it must be. And from the way he'd reacted, the woman had been the one doing the breaking, and he the one being broken.

She couldn't help secretly admitting to herself she was glad that woman was no longer on the scene, even if it meant Chase had been hurt. Hearts, she knew, might be broken, but eventually they found a way to mend, and even if never fully intact, managed to function and even thrive eventually.

They ate in silence for a while. Chase's color returned to normal, and he commented on how delicious the food was. "I don't know if I'll have room for the streusel," he said. "But I know I'll enjoy watching you eat it."

Kate laughed, slightly embarrassed by his remark, and at the same time aroused by his tone and the spark in his eyes. She was glad he'd mastered whatever pain had gripped him as a result of her question. Though she wanted to know more, she understood now wasn't the time to probe.

Instead, she decided to share something of herself. "I had my heart broken too," she offered, thereby subtly letting him know she understood his pain. When he didn't refute her implied assumption, she continued, "His name was Victor. Ironically, we had our falling out over BDSM too, only that time it wasn't because he took me too far, it was because I wanted more than he was able to give. He just wanted to play, and when it got serious for me, he freaked out and ran." She gave a small laugh and shrugged. "I don't seem too good at picking out play partners in the scene. In fact, I'd say I'm O for two."

She glanced at Chase, and was taken aback by the intensity of his gaze. His eyes were smoldering and she felt his power, just as she'd felt Master John's. It was something primal that needed no language. She felt herself yielding to it, melting against it. She tried to look away, but found herself locked to the blue flames in his eyes, as surely as a moth is drawn to its sweet, fiery death.

Kate again felt her nipples rise, and her pussy was suddenly swollen and aching between her legs. She hadn't planned on falling for this guy, but she could no longer deny the magnetic pull of their mutual attraction.

"Maybe," Chase said softly, "the third time's the charm."

Chapter 10

"So, what did you mean, the third time's the charm?"

Chase grinned at the cell phone, delighted that Kate had called, amused that she'd barely said hello before diving in with that question.

It was the evening after their lunch date. Chase had been hoping Kate would invite him back to her place when they'd finished the meal, but she hadn't, claiming she had to finish a chapter on her manuscript, though he'd sensed there was more at play.

He'd made the drive back to the city, musing over the intense attraction he'd felt, not only for her, but from her as the lunch had progressed. At the same time, he could see she was conflicted about delving deeper into BDSM with someone new, and he couldn't blame her, after what she'd been through.

"I meant that I don't think your issue is with D/s per se, but just with your choice of a partner so far. You need someone who understands your need to submit, but who also cherishes you. Someone who is confident and secure as a Dom, not afraid to take you where you need to go, but also sensitive to your limits."

Kate laughed. "Oh, and this is where you tell me you're that guy." Her tone was teasing.

"I just might be," Chase replied seriously, as Lisa's already loosening grip on his heart eased just a little more. "I guess that depends on you. On us. It's a matter of trust, Kate. And that's something that's earned." As he said this, Chase realized he wasn't only talking about his potential role as her Dom. He needed to learn to trust himself again as well.

The exciting thing was, he felt ready. It was as if he'd been through a long winter, his feelings dormant beneath the ice of regret and loss. Now the thaw had come, in the guise of Kate's bright, sunny countenance, her teasing banter, her lovely body. He was awakening after a self-imposed hibernation, and he wanted to live again, fully.

He wanted to love again.

The way she'd put her wrists together, as if asking to be bound then and there at the café, had sent a jolt of longing through Chase's being. He wanted to be the one to teach her, to help her explore her submissive nature. He wanted to claim her for his own.

Slow down, Saunders. Slow way the fuck down.

Never one to rush into anything, especially not a new relationship, he reminded himself of the sometimes insidious power of infatuation. The incredibly intense, wonderful and all-consuming feelings of something new could easily fade when the relationship moved beyond the early, superficial connection. He owed it to both Kate and himself to take it slowly.

They talked a while longer, about D/s in general and their potential connection in particular. Chase tried to keep the tone light, not wanting to scare Kate away with the intensity of his feelings on the matter. He teased her, delighted when she giggled, the sound rife with a silly joy that made him remember life didn't always have to be so fucking serious.

When they'd hung up, he sat a long while, just thinking. "You know what?" he finally said aloud. "Maybe my problem is I do take things too damn slow. By the time I'm ready to move, the opportunity is lost. Maybe...just maybe it's time to do it different."

~*~

Kate spent the morning with her editor, going over the final revisions to her latest manuscript at the offices of her publisher. Though they mostly worked by email, both enjoyed meeting face to face from time to time, and agreed it improved their working relationship to do so.

She'd driven into the city, something she didn't usually do, normally taking the train. Chase had offered to pick her up after her meeting at her publisher's and drive her to his place in Queens, but Kate had preferred to drive. This way she'd be able to leave his place when she wanted — she'd be in control.

She was excited at the prospect of seeing his rope making business and the bondage room where he held private workshops and perhaps where he bound his lovers. Mostly, she was excited at the prospect of seeing *him*.

He'd given her very precise directions, and she concentrated on them, being what friends teasingly called "directionally impaired".

It had been nearly a week since their lunch. They had talked several more times on the phone since then, sometimes teasing, sometimes serious. She'd shared more about her feelings, and he'd talked about his experience as well, though always in an abstract way — no names, no details. That girl in the video had definitely done a serious number on Chase, and Kate had nearly asked several times just what had happened between them, but never quite found the nerve. She only hoped he wasn't too hung up by whatever happened to try again.

Just the same, she found herself increasingly eager to see him again. She wanted to see his dark blue eyes crinkling at the corners when he smiled. She wanted to feel the heat he'd caused by gazing at her with such fierce intensity, whispering without words that he wanted her — more than that, that he wanted to claim her.

Used to guys who came on too strong, she found herself intrigued by Chase's apparent contentment to take things slowly. As they got to know each other better over the phone, she understood his caution wasn't based on fear or insecurity, but rather from a real desire to get to know her. He wasn't just looking for a new conquest, but really seemed to want to know her as a person.

Chase's house was located in the Jackson Heights neighborhood of Queens. It was a two story brick house that looked rather small, but well tended. Kate was charmed by the window boxes on all four windows facing the street, each filled with brightly colored flowers. The yard was the size of a postage stamp, but the grass was neatly mowed, bifurcated by a stone path that led to his front door.

She lifted the small brass knocker in the center of the front door and let it fall twice. A moment later Chase pulled open the door, greeting her with a radiant, dimpled smile. Though he wasn't as tall or powerfully built as Master John, he was fit, his shoulders broad, his legs muscular. She hadn't been initially attracted to him at the weekend, but she realized now it was because she was so distracted and excited by Master John and what he seemed to offer, that she'd missed Chase's more subtle appeal.

"Kate, you look beautiful." Chase leaned forward to kiss her cheek. Kate smiled, pleased with his compliment, and stepped inside his house.

That morning when she'd showered and dressed, she'd selected her new pale pink lace bra and panty set from *Victoria's Secret* that she'd bought a month before, but had yet to wear. She'd had a small argument with herself as she dressed, reminding herself this wasn't a date, it was just a nice guy showing her around his bondage shop, at her request.

And yet she'd put on the pretty underwear, shivering as she imagined Chase's hands moving over her skin. Still she tried to fool herself, recalling the article in a women's magazine she'd read that said nice underwear beneath your clothing would make you feel more confident. That was all she was doing—boosting her confidence.

"It's hot out there. Let me get you something cold to drink. Then, if you want, I'll give you the garage tour of my cottage industry."

Though the house was small, Kate was aware of the astronomical real estate prices, even thirty minutes out of Manhattan. "There must be a huge demand for your rope, to be able to live in this neighborhood," she remarked. The small foyer opened onto a living room, which was sparsely furnished with two blue and white striped loveseats facing one another across a dark blue rug in front of a stone fireplace. There was also a large, comfortable looking leather recliner of caramel-colored leather, a small table beside it piled with books. The floors were hardwood and looked freshly varnished.

"I wish," Chase said with a smile. "I'm doing well, but I doubt I could afford this place on my own. I confess I inherited it from my Aunt Polly, who lived here her entire adult life, buying back in 1959 when Queens was still considered quite a trip from Manhattan, instead of an express subway ride away. My sister got the beach house in Long Island, which worked out, since she loves the water and has little kids. Polly never married, and I guess my sister and me lucked out as a result. I miss her though. She was a hoot. She was actually into the scene."

"No way. How'd you find that out?"

"When I cleaned out the attic. She had a huge stash of bondage gear and equipment stored up there. The room I've taken over as my bondage playroom was already fitted with eyehooks in the ceiling and floor, and various other telltale indications it'd been used as more than the guest bedroom. Family lore had it that she was a massage therapist, but it's pretty clear she did way more than rub out the kinks. She was a professional Dominatrix, I'm nearly certain. She was seventy-four when she died of a stroke, but I wouldn't be surprised if she was actively into the scene to the end."

Kate laughed. "That's wild. Well, I guess it makes sense. Who says one's kink has a time limit?" *My bondage playroom*...The words echoed in her mind. Was it there he'd tied down the woman in red, before making love to her? Kate shook away the thought.

She followed Chase into a small, old-fashioned kitchen, most of it taken up by a large gas range and a round wooden breakfast table in the corner.

"Lemonade okay? Or I have water or beer."

"Lemonade sounds perfect," Kate said, watching as he pulled two tumblers from the cabinet and filled them. She liked the way his forearms looked, muscular and tan beneath the sleeves rolled to three-quarters just below his elbow.

He handed her a glass and took a long drink from his own. He gestured toward the table, indicating she should sit. Kate noticed the vase of fresh flowers at its center. A woman's touch? Or was she being sexist.

"Nice flowers," she said, subtly fishing for the answer.

"Thanks. I like to keep fresh cut flowers in the house during spring and summer. I grow them out back. No lawn to mow, the whole thing is a garden. I'd like to put in a vegetable garden too but never got around to it. Maybe next spring."

There was a certain wistfulness to Chase's tone, and he stared out the window, though somehow Kate doubted he was looking at the view. Enough pussyfooting around. She asked outright, "So, do you live alone here?"

He took a moment to answer, as if lost in a daydream. Whipping his head toward her, he said, "What? Oh, yes. Alone."

"I do too," she offered, feeling a little stupid. "Your place is so tidy and, you know, with those flowers and all, I figured maybe…"

Chase lifted his eyebrows and grinned. "You're assuming a guy can't possibly keep his house neat and enjoy a bright spray of flowers on his kitchen table, is that what I'm hearing?" His voice was teasing, but his words hit home.

"I guess in my limited experience, men are, for the most part, slobs." She offered an apologetic grin.

"I'll accept that but, for the record, so, for the most part, are women. I like order. I like things put away where they belong. There is a time for abandon, of course, for letting things go a little wild. I find that more in the emotional realm." He leaned across the table, his voice lowering suddenly as he reached out and stroked Kate's bare arm, sending an actual shiver of desire through her body.

"What about you, Kate? Can you let go? Have you ever given yourself over to someone else, without stopping to think how you look or what he might think or how something is supposed to make you feel?"

The shift in mood caught her by surprise. She felt her cheeks heating and turned away. "I—I don't know what you mean," she protested feebly.

"Don't you?"

Kate pushed back from the table and stood, turning back to face him. *Had* she ever done that? Given herself over without stopping to analyze every possible aspect of the scenario? She'd had all the scenes with Victor scripted in her head, and had pretty much directed the show, since she was supposedly the one "into the scene" and he was just going along.

Even with Master John, they'd carefully negotiated the scene, and she'd listed a litany of boundaries he wasn't to cross, though in the end he'd ignored them all. "If you mean have I ever engaged in an exchange of erotic power, where I gave complete control to another person, without first negotiating my limits and boundaries, no. No I haven't."

Chase stood too and nodded, his eyes burning into hers. "I sense something in you, Kate. Something powerful and sensual that you've never explored, maybe that you don't even know is there. But I believe you. I understand you've never given yourself completely and from what you've told me and what I've observed, that's a good thing. You've never been in an intimate situation, at least as far as BDSM is concerned, where a solid foundation of trust had been established. As we've talked about on the phone, that's the key. You can never fully submit to another person unless you trust them with your very life. For that, quite literally, is what you put into their hands."

They were standing very close. Chase took her face in his hands. "You can trust me, Kate," he whispered. "That I promise you." He kissed her, his lips just a press against hers at first, soft and warm. She parted her lips and he teased along the parting with his tongue. She sighed against him, encircling his neck with her hands, hungry for his touch.

He wrapped her in strong arms, pulling her close until her breasts were pressed against his firm chest. She felt herself falling, then and there, into a new level of desire, of longing for not only what Chase offered, but for the man himself.

He was the first to pull away, gently disengaging himself from her arms. "Don't you want to see the rope factory?" His tone was light, a teasing smile on his lips, though the bulging erection in his jeans gave him away.

Kate was aware they were moving toward something more, much more, than just a guided tour of his rope business but she was content to wait a little longer, if that's what he wanted.

"Sure." She grinned. "It's your fault. You distracted me." She shook her hair back from her face. "Lead the way."

Chase led her out the kitchen door, through the riot of color in his flower gardens, to the detached garage. Inside were a number of large kettles resting on huge gas burners. Literally miles of rope in varying hues and thicknesses were hung along the walls and rested in coils along counters on either side of the space. Chase lifted his arms, doing a slow circle. "This is it. The bondage rope shop. Not exactly glamorous, huh? Actually it's sweaty, dirty business, but the end product is worth all the work."

"What are all those kettles for?" Kate asked.

"That's where we boil the raw hemp and do the dyeing. Remember how rough that untreated rope was? I start off by boiling it to soften it. I treat it with oils and color it with dyes."

Kate moved toward one of the counters and picked up a length of bright yellow rope, not yet coiled. She fingered it, a thrill of desire pinging inside her. "It's not as soft as the rope you gave me at lunch." She'd taken that coil home and unwrapped it, winding it around and around her wrists in the privacy of her own bed, wondering what it would be like to scene with Chase. Though she hadn't admitted it to Chase of course, she'd made herself come with the rope still entwined around her wrists.

"That's because the coil I gave you is from my own personal stash. What you're holding now is new. High quality hemp rope is kind of like a good pair of blue jeans. It starts out slightly stiff to the touch, but becomes softer and suppler with each use. As you work with the rope, the fibers relax until it becomes like a second skin.

"For bondage play, at least as I practice it, the idea isn't to cut into the skin or cause discomfort, or even about restraint, per se. For me, rope is all about connection, the strands of hemp an extension of your desire for the other person, a way of wrapping them, protecting them while you take them on a journey to where they need to go."

Kate absorbed this, unable to help contrasting this in her mind to Master John's use of restraint—painful metal cuffs that cut into her wrists when she struggled, despite their lining. Whatever journey he'd been on, she hadn't been a part of it, except as an object for his aggression.

She continued to stroke the yellow rope, wondering what it would feel like to be "wrapped" by Chase, and taken where she needed to go.

"So, how about a tour of your bondage playroom, the one where you're carrying on the family tradition?"

Chase smiled, but shoved his hands into his pockets and angled slightly away from her. "Oh," he said, still not looking at her. "I haven't been in there in a while."

Kate waited, not sure what he meant. Was he saying no? Then suddenly it clicked. The girl in red. He probably hadn't been in there since they'd broken up. Emboldened by his kiss, and tired of dancing around the issue he obviously wasn't going to bring up on his own, Kate blurted, "You keep talking about trust, but isn't that a two-way street? When are you going to trust *me* enough to let me in? At least a little?"

Chase turned back to her with a stricken look. "You're right. I'm sorry. It's just…it's been a while. You're the first…I mean, I haven't…" He took a breath and blew it out. Putting his face in his hands, he moved them over it like he was washing it, and continued up through his hair.

Finally he dropped his hands and looked at her. "I apologize. And you're right. Trust is a two-way street. I owe you more of an explanation." His voice dipped to where it was nearly inaudible. "Her name was Lisa."

There was a pause, during which Kate tried not to tap her foot with impatience. Did he think he was the first person ever to be dumped? At the same time she felt a stab of compassion for what he must be going through. She'd been devastated when Victor had walked out, convinced she'd never get over him or what he'd done in rejecting the trust she'd dared to place in him.

Time, she wanted to tell Chase, really does heal even the most shattered of hearts. But she said nothing, sensing such words would be received as trite advice. Instead she waited while he composed himself.

"I'm sorry. I'm just not ready to talk about it yet. I want to—I will, I promise. If you could just give me a while longer. I want you, Kate. The past doesn't matter."

As he looked at her his beseeching gaze slowly changed into something quite different. As had happened at the café, Kate found herself falling into his dark blue eyes, which drew her with a power that skipped past words and went straight to the core of her being. Kate forgot about the woman in red. She forgot about her own nerves at the thought of starting something new. She forgot about everything except how much she wanted him to kiss her again.

He held out his hands and she moved closer, lost in his fiery gaze. He pulled her into his arms, drawing her against his chest. He held her tight, after a moment lifting one hand to stroke her hair. "Thank you," he whispered, "for your trust."

Chapter 11

Had it really been a year since he'd gone into this room?

It wasn't that he'd meant to stay away so long, it had just happened. Since Lisa, he'd had no interest in casual scenes with the women he met at the workshops and seminars he conducted, though he'd had plenty of offers.

It wasn't that he'd lost his passion for sensual bondage and erotic BDSM play. He still loved it as much as ever—the feel of the rope artfully knotted against smooth skin, the softening of a woman's features when lust and submission overtook her, his own power when he claimed control of not only her body, but her spirit. He loved that still—it was a part of what and who he was.

It was just that he'd lost his interest in any *specific* woman.

Until now.

Chase took Kate's hand and led her back into the house. He was aching for this woman in a way that was new to him. Not even with Lisa at the height of their passion had he felt this kind of burning longing, like molten lava ready to gush over the lip of a volcano of denied feelings. They walked through the living room to the narrow, steep stairs that led to the second floor of the old house.

As they entered the room, he watched Kate, her mouth dropping open slightly as her eyes flitted over the space, taking it all in. He'd painted the walls a deep, rich blue, a color he found calming. Unlit white candles lined a high shelf that ran the perimeter of the room, some of them nearly melted away to stumps. He made a mental note to replace them.

The free standing suspension rig rested against one wall, ready to be set up for instant, portable suspension play. He'd designed it from aluminum pipes, welded together into a triangle, perfect for any number of suspension positions, both upright and upside down, legs spread wide. Against another wall were coils of rope of various thicknesses and lengths, dyed in deep red, blue and black. Hung along a third wall, beneath the large window, was his cache of whips, canes, floggers and crops.

In the center of the room, stainless steel suspension rings were firmly secured into a wooden beam in the ceiling, with ropes from each threaded through a pulley mechanism that operated from a winch set into the wall.

Kate was turning slowly, her eyes wide, her hands clutched at her chest. "Gosh," she said, the single word laden with wonder and awe. "This is amazing."

Her gaze fell on the safety shears, which hung on a large red hook on the wall just inside the door. "What are those for?"

Forcing his lust down, Chase focused on her question. "Those are EMT shears, or some people refer to them as bandage shears. The edges are blunted so you can press it safely against the skin without danger of cutting the person's flesh. It's a must-have safety tool for anyone doing rope bondage, because if anything goes wrong, from a muscle cramp to the house catching on fire, you have to be able to get someone untied quickly and safely."

Kate nodded. "That makes sense."

"Yeah. I think one of the scariest days of my life was back in college. I was just messing around with bondage back then, still learning the ropes." He grinned while Kate grimaced at his pun. "Anyway this girl I had tied up suddenly started passing out. Turns out she was on some kind of stupid diet and hadn't eaten anything but grapefruit and lettuce for like three days. Those were the longest, scariest thirty seconds of my life, trying to get her untied and into a safe position."

"I guess I should be glad Master John used cuffs and not rope, huh? All you had to do was turn the keys."

Chase winced. "Ah, Kate, I'm sorry. I didn't mean to make you think of that."

"It's okay. I'm all right, really. No more nightmares. I learned my lesson. I'm just lucky you were there. I never really thanked you for what you did. So, thank you. You were my knight in shining honor."

Chase laughed. "I don't know about that. I didn't handle myself so well, if you want to know. In fact,

Brighton and I got into a fist fight. We knocked over one of the screens in the process, caused a ruckus and got a stern talking to. I doubt Power Play will be asking me back anytime soon."

"Chase! I had no idea. And it's because of me." Kate exclaimed. "Because I made a bad choice."

"No," Chase said firmly. "It's because Brighton was an ass who stepped way over the line and had to be reined in. Now, let's not talk about that anymore. Come here." He reached for her, and she allowed him to draw her into his arms.

They kissed again, and Chase felt the slow burn of desire curling through his body. Pulling back, he reached for her arms and lifted them, guiding her hands to the O ring hanging from the ceiling. Taking his cue, she gripped it, swaying slightly.

"Will it support my weight?" she asked, her voice tremulous.

"Oh, yes, absolutely," Chase assured her. His cock was aching, fully erect and pointing toward his left hip. He stepped behind her, reaching up to grasp her wrists. She didn't release her hold of the ring, but stood still, as if already bound. Chase leaned forward, pressing his body against hers, feeling the curve of her ass against his cock. She didn't pull away.

His mouth next to her ear, he murmured, "Would you like for me to give you a taste of sensual bondage?" He ran his fingers lightly down her arms, moving along the silky fabric that covered her torso, feeling the slight tremor in her body as he touched her.

"Yes, please," she said throatily.

When he moved to retrieve the proper rope, Chase realized his owns hands were trembling slightly, with both excitement and perhaps a bit of fear.

It had been so long.

He wasn't worried about his skill with the various intricate knots that he used or his ability with a flogger or cane, but was his touch still sure? Did he still have what it took to dominate a woman, to make her shudder and moan with desire, to make her surrender her body and her will?

He used a basic two column tie on her wrists, securing her with the soft rope. The room was relatively cool, compared with the summer heat outside, but Kate's skin was hot to the touch. His lips itched to kiss her again, but he forced himself to focus on his task.

"How's that?" he asked, stepping back to appraise his handiwork. He'd chosen the royal blue rope, which looked pretty against her pale, smooth skin and contrasted nicely with her coppery red hair. "Are you comfortable?" Kate's cheeks were flushed, making her eyes look even greener, a deep, clear emerald green with tiny flecks of gold around the pupils.

She pulled against the rope. "Yes." She swallowed and took a deep, shuddery breath. She was fidgeting, moving her feet in a nervous little dance on the floor.

He stroked her cheek and spoke gently, caressing her the way one might gentle a wild horse. "Relax. You're safe. We're just experimenting right now. I'm going to take off your sandals. And then I'm going to raise the pulley, just a little, just enough to put you on tiptoe, but not high enough for full suspension, okay?"

Kate nodded, visibly swallowing again. Chase knelt and slipped the sandals from her pretty, slender feet. He noticed her toenails were painted a pale pink, like the inner part of a nautilus shell. Standing, he moved toward the wall, taking the long blue rope with him and threading it through the winch. He turned the handle slowly, watching as she was forced higher, rising on tiptoe, her arms stretched taut.

Returning to the bound girl, he lightly kissed her cheek. "Is this what you want, Kate? Is it what you need?" He ran his hands down her sides again, barely touching the swell of her breasts as his hands moved past them.

She nodded. Her nipples were poking against the thin fabric of her blouse.

"Say it, Kate. Tell me what you need." Though he'd meant to go slow, Chase felt his natural dominance rising to the fore. Something about the rope, something about the knots and the steel, coupled with her beauty and vulnerability, all triggered that primal urge to assert his mastery that was never too far below the surface.

"Tell me." Chase fixed his gaze on hers. He felt energized—alive—for the first time in ages. He rocked on the balls of his feet, lust and power zipping through his body like electrical currents. Jesus, he wanted this woman.

"I want..." Kate began. She took a breath and continued. "I need...this. I need to feel the rope against my wrists, my body pulled taut. It just feels so...right. I don't know how else to say it."

"I understand. And it is right. Just right for you, and for me." He moved closer and pushed the tendrils of hair out of her face, tenderness and raw lust warring inside him. Kate was wearing a pale blue sleeveless blouse with tiny buttons down its front, several of them opened at her throat. Chase squelched the desire to grip the fabric on either side of her collar and rip it open, letting the little buttons spray over the floor so he could bury his face between the luscious mounds of flesh.

"I want you," he murmured, before realizing he'd said the words aloud.

"Kiss me," she replied.

~*~

When he stepped back from the kiss, Kate realized she was panting. The feeling of the rope, wound and knotted securely around her wrists, was incredible. She loved the way her body was stretched, her back arched, breasts thrust forward, nipples achingly erect.

All that was missing, she realized, was the feel of leather stroking her flesh, moving over her skin. "What?" Chase asked, watching her face. "What is it you want, Kate? Tell me."

"The flogger," she begged, too aroused to be shy.

Chase raised his eyebrows. "Are you sure? This was just a demonstration. A taste, if you will. Do you think you're ready to be flogged while so thoroughly restrained?"

"I want it," she asserted, adding afterwards a belated, "please."

Chase laughed. "All right then. You shall have it. But I can't flog you with all these clothes covering you. We'll have to remove the skirt, at least."

Kate nodded, recalling the pretty pink lace panties she was wearing, aware on some level she'd known, one way or the other, that Chase would end up seeing them. Chase moved behind her and unzipped the skirt, letting it fall to her feet. She stepped out of it and he picked it up and hung it on a spare hook beside the whips and floggers.

He selected a flogger, a large one with thick, soft-looking tresses, and approached her again. "You sure about this, Kate? You can still change your mind."

"I'm sure," she whispered, aware of the throbbing ache between her legs and the rapid tattoo of her heartbeat.

Chase nodded and moved behind her. "Your safeword is lemon, though I doubt you'll have need of it. I'm going to start very gently. We'll take our time." Kate shuddered slightly as he drew the smooth leather tresses over her ass and trailed them along her thighs. He let it strike her with a whisper of a sting, and then slid it sensually along her skin again.

"Spread your legs," he ordered, a quiet steel in his voice that hadn't been there a moment before. He moved to stand beside her and faced her. Suspended as she was, Kate couldn't move too much, though by rising higher on her toes she was able to move a little. She swayed in her bonds, startled and aroused when Chase, one hand in front of her, one hand behind, drew the whip between her legs, passing it along her swollen labia.

"Have you ever been flogged, Kate? Properly flogged?" His voice was a low, sensual purr.

"Not properly," she answered, knowing it was true, certain he could give her what she'd been seeking, but with the wrong men.

Chase moved in front of her, tucking the flogger under one arm. "I'm going to open your blouse, Kate." It was a statement, not a question, and it didn't occur to Kate to protest. He kept his eyes on her face while he unbuttoned the blouse, revealing her pink lace bra.

His eyes flickered down then, and they were hooded with lust. "Beautiful," he whispered. "Perfect." He moved again to her right side and ran the whip's tresses between her breasts and down her abdomen. He drew it up between her legs, pulling up until she felt the tug of the leather against her sex.

"Please," she begged, not entirely sure what she was begging for, but aching for it nonetheless.

He moved again behind her. This time the kiss of leather carried a sting, though just enough to heat her skin. She leaned back into the stroke of the flogger as it landed again and again on her ass, only just hard enough to make its presence felt.

She wanted more, but didn't ask for it, letting him set the pace and intensity. As her skin became more sensitive, the sting made itself felt, edging from just a brushing of skin into the realm of erotic pain.

"Yes," she moaned, aching for more. Victor had never understood this need for the pain, thinking of it only in terms of punishment, of suffering. But it went far beyond that for Kate. Or she knew it could, with the right person to lead her there.

Chase paid attention, because the strokes came harder now, a steady series of stinging blows that made Kate dance on her toes, swaying as she gripped the steel ring high over her head. "Oh, oh, oh…" She could feel herself hovering on the edge of something, moving toward a place she needed to be, if only she could get past the stinging pain.

"How're you doing?" Chase asked, stopping to stroke her heated flesh with cool, sure fingers. "Do you want me to continue?"

"Yes, please," she murmured. *Yes, yes, yes, yes!* He stroked her a while longer and then stepped back, flogger in hand. "Ah!" she cried, the blow coming so hard she lost her footing, her weight completely on her wrists for a moment until she righted herself.

"Do I go on, Kate? Have you had enough?"

"More," she begged, surprised at how ragged, how needy, her voice sounded to her own ears. *This* was what she wanted, what she had sought when she'd agreed to the scene with Master John.

Chase resumed the flogging, covering her ass and the backs of her thighs with a fire of leather, almost too much to bear, but only almost. Kate was panting, small, bleating moans escaping her lips, coming in time with each strike of the flogger.

It's too much...too much...oh god...oh no...oh yes...oooooooh....

The oddest thing began to happen. The panic edging the pain slowly leached away as an odd, heavy kind of peace took its place. Her fingers, which had been tightly curled around the steel ring, eased and loosened. She sagged against her bonds and her head fell back, her mouth hanging open. She tried to close it, but couldn't muster the will.

She was floating, barely conscious, or rather, she was conscious but in an almost trancelike state. A dreamy erotic sort of floating sensation had overtaken both her body and her mind.

Chase continued to flog her, but she no longer felt the sting. It was more of a kiss, the swish and thwack of leather stroking her deeper and deeper into the heavenly trance. *I'm flying,* she realized dimly, as she soared. This was what she'd read about, but never really understood. It was...*perfect*...

~*~

Chase put down the flogger and lowered Kate until her feet were firmly on the ground. Her head was back, the long, beautiful hair streaming down. Her lips were parted, eyes closed, a look of utter bliss on her face.

He knew where she was—he had taken Lisa there many times, but not until they'd been together several months. He was amazed to see where Kate had gone, so quickly, and with someone so new.

Though his cock and balls were aching, he forced himself to focus. Deftly he released the knots that bound her wrists, supporting her as she sagged against him. Chase cradled her in his arms, feeling at once on fire with lust and achingly tender toward this new woman in his life.

Was she in his life? Was he ready for another relationship? Would Lisa let go of his heart at last?

Kate slowly opened her eyes and smiled dreamily at him. "Wow," she said softly. "Where was I?"

"Right where you needed to be," Chase answered.

Chapter 12

Kate leaned heavily into Chase as they moved from the bondage room along the hall toward his bedroom. He put a steadying arm around her as they walked, guiding her. He took her into the master bedroom, leading her to the large bed, which was set in a four poster wrought iron frame.

She sat at the bottom of the bed, perched on the edge, a look of dreamy contentment on her face. "Gosh, Chase. That was amazing. I've never experienced anything like it. I guess that's what they call flying, huh?"

Chase knelt on the rug in front of Kate and put his hands on her bare thighs. "Yeah. It's really something to watch, to be a part of. There's no greater high for a Dom than taking his sub there. It's..." He paused, trying to come up with the right words to capture what was, essentially, indescribable. "...it's a moment of intense connection. There is no other time, or place, or past or future. Everything is completely concentrated in that moment. It's like a beam of light as focused as a laser, and as powerful." He laughed at himself. "I know I'm making absolutely no sense."

"No, no, you are. I mean, I experienced that too — the connectedness. Like the flogger was an extension of your arm, like you were," she paused and ducked her head, finishing shyly, "making love to me with it." She laughed. "Now who's making no sense?"

"It makes perfect sense," Chase murmured, stroking her impossibly soft skin. "It's about trust. I could feel your trust and that freed me to take you further on the journey. You give me the power, you see, when you give me that trust. That's what I mean about an erotic exchange of power. When it happens, there's nothing like it. I take that gift very seriously, Kate. And I would never abuse it."

"Thank you," Kate whispered.

"Thank you," he responded, "for your gift." He looked down at his hands, still resting on her thighs. They were tan against her pale skin. He moved them slowly upward, toward her panties, spreading her legs as he moved.

"Oh," Kate said, putting her hands on top of his, as if to stop him. He looked at her. Her nipples were hard points through the lace of her bra, and her eyes were wide. He understood her hesitation—moving past a bondage scene to something much more intimate was a lot for the mind to handle, even if the body wanted it. Yet he could feel her desire radiating like shimmering heat moving over her skin.

"Do you want me to stop, Kate? I want to go on. I want to touch you, to stroke you. To continue the lovemaking we began back in the bondage room. Would that suit you?"

"Yes," she whispered. "Please. Yes."

He leaned up and kissed Kate's lips, a long lingering kiss. She brought her arms around his neck, kissing him back, their tongues intertwining, her breath coming faster. When at last they fell away from each other, Chase leaned back again on his haunches.

He again moved his hands, letting the tips of his fingers graze the lace-covered heat between her legs. Kate's lips were parted, her eyes shining.

"Lie back on the bed, Kate. I want to look at you." Kate didn't obey, but nor did she close her legs or try to cover herself. She was nervous, he could see, but she wanted this as much as he did, he was pretty sure. Gently he pushed at one shoulder and Kate yielded, lying back on the mattress, her hair a fiery copper storm against the dark blue of his duvet.

Chase drank in her beauty. He reached for the buttons on his shirt, undoing them, his eyes on Kate's lovely body. It had been so long since he'd been inside a woman, embraced and stroked, held tight as she shuddered and sighed beneath him. When Lisa was in one of her depressions, which was more often than not toward the end, she wouldn't allow Chase to touch her, except with rope and leather. Though she craved the kiss of the lash, she refused sex, claiming it hurt her to be penetrated when she wasn't relaxed.

But when she was happy, high on the upside of the seesaw of her mood swings, sex with her was phenomenal — they would work themselves into a frenzy of delight, a soaring wet ecstasy of orgasmic abandon that left them both utterly spent, pinned to the bed by sheer exhaustion.

Dear heart, I miss you.

For a split second Chase thought the words had been spoken aloud in Lisa's distinctive, rather girlish voice. Of course that was impossible and he refused to indulge the strong impulse to turn around just to make sure she wasn't standing there.

Dear heart. That had been one of their many secret jokes, the kind shared between a couple who has been together for a long time. When she'd first used the endearment, for some reason he'd thought she was saying "deer heart" and was bewildered as to why she would call him that. It had become a running joke between them, for him to reply, "Yes, doe heart?"

"Chase?" Kate had propped herself on one elbow. She stared at him with watchful eyes. "Are you okay?" She frowned.

Damn it, he was doing a great job of ruining the intense, sexy mood of a moment before, he thought darkly. Forcing the unwelcome memories aside, he leaned down, kissing Kate's bare thigh as he placed his hands on either one.

"I'm fine. Better than fine."

Kate fell back against the bed, watching Chase through half-closed eyes, her arms flung loosely at her sides, her legs spread just enough so he could see the alluring swell of her pussy barely hidden in pink lace.

Chase pulled off his shirt, tossing it aside as he leaned over Kate, intent on kissing her. She reached for him.

He held himself carefully at first, not wanting to crush her beneath his weight. But she pulled him down, wrapping her long, strong legs around his back until he was resting his full weight on top of her. They kissed, lips parting, tongues dancing, hearts beating fast. He felt as if he were drinking her in, and she was the purest clear water for a man who had been, literally, dying of thirst — the thirst for love and connection he'd denied himself for so long.

He extracted himself from the ardent tangle of her legs and arms just long enough to pull off his jeans and underwear. His cock sprang free, the tip already wet with pre-cum. Kate lifted her head slightly, licking her lips as she stared brazenly at his naked body.

Chase's cock got even harder, if that was possible. She was just what he loved — a strong, sexy woman who knew what she wanted. Laying claim to such a woman in a D/s relationship was infinitely more satisfying than domming someone who was passive and insecure. He wanted her, oh god, how he wanted her.

Kneeling before her, he hooked his fingers into the waistband of her panties at either hip and dragged them down. Kate lifted her ass helpfully, her eyes sparkling with lust. He reached around her to release the tiny hooks that held her bra closed.

He pulled it from her body and knelt again in front of Kate. Her breasts were every bit as beautiful as he'd imagined, the rosy pink nipples stiff against the creamy white globes. She reached for him, but he didn't let her pull him down this time. Instead his eyes lingered over her bare body, moving from her breasts to her pubic mound, which was sparsely covered with reddish blond pubic hair. Placing a hand on each of her thighs, gently he spread her legs.

She resisted at first, and he said, "I want to see you. Don't deny me, Kate." Though he did very much want to see her lovely pussy, this was also a test of sorts, to see how far his sway over her still held, after the scene in the bondage room.

He was pleased when she relaxed her muscles and allowed him to part her legs. Her pussy was small, the labia beautifully formed, reminding him of a newly budding rose. He leaned close, inhaling her intoxicating, womanly scent. He kissed her inner left thigh, his lips trailing over the satiny soft skin.

He kissed the other thigh, moving upward toward her pussy. The inner labia were swollen and glistening with her juices. Gently he touched the tip of his tongue to the soft, sensual folds.

Kate shuddered and sighed. He licked in long, slow lines up and down the sweet petals of her sex, purposefully avoiding the hard nubbin at her center, which was dark red and swollen. Kate moaned and shifted, clearly trying to angle herself to get what she wanted.

He felt her long, slender fingers on either side of his head. The wanton girl was trying to guide him! With a low growl of a laugh, Chase grabbed her hands in his and pinned her arms on either side of her body against the mattress.

"Oooh," Kate breathed. Her nipples were hard points. He leaned forward and licked and lightly bit each one, drawing a moan with each caress and pull. He loved the feel of her nipples, like soft marbles against his teeth and tongue, but he didn't linger too long, eager to taste her spicy sweetness again. Still holding her wrists, he moved down along her body with his lips and tongue, tasting the salt on her skin. He moved over her pubic mound, this time circling her hard clit with his tongue.

Kate jerked against the restraint of his hands on her wrists. He gripped her tighter as he licked and teased her until she was moaning and writhing beneath him.

"Fuck me," she breathed.

Chase didn't need to be asked twice. He rose and hurried to his bureau, where he rummaged in his underwear drawer for a condom. He slid it quickly over his erection and returned to the bed.

Again leaning over the lovely girl, he kissed her lips and throat, licking over the smooth skin, lightly nipping her nipples with his teeth until he felt her soften and relax beneath him.

Wrapping his arms around her, he lifted her along the mattress, settling her so she was resting her head against the pillows. Kneeling on the bed between her thighs, he focused again on her pussy, wet and sticky from her juices and his kisses. He licked and suckled her until she was again moaning and arching toward him.

"Ah," she begged, "Fuck me. *Please.*"

There was such sweet yearning in her tone that he didn't want to refuse her another second. He was stone hard, his balls tight with need. Standing over her, he lowered himself on the bed, holding his weight with his arms on either side of her. He touched the head of his cock to her wetness and pressed carefully into her. Again the strong legs came around him, pulling him in deeper.

She kissed his mouth, focused on his lower lip, which she sucked in between hers. He found this strange half-kiss deeply erotic and surrendered himself to it, and to the tight, hot clench of her pussy, which spasmed around him as Kate moaned against his mouth.

Kate was clinging to Chase now, and where a moment before she had been moving in a pulsing, sensual rhythm beneath him, she suddenly stiffened, her body rigid beneath his, her heart thumping against his chest. "Oh, oh, oh..." She began to pant, her body still rigid, her cunt spasming hard against his cock.

She was coming, coming on his cock, her fingers digging into his shoulders. It felt so good, so amazingly wonderfully good and he felt himself moving with her, all the pain and longing of the last year sluiced away with the gush of semen shooting from his shaft.

"Oh shit, oh god," he whispered between clenched teeth, his body flooding with pleasure as he climaxed. "Oh, Lisa, yes!" he cried, realizing only a split second after the words had left his mouth, just whose name he'd called.

~*~

Kate lay still beneath Chase. He was sweating lightly, his chest crushing her breasts, his cock still hard inside her. The pleasure of Kate's orgasm, the lingering thrill of the scene in the bondage room, all of it melted away at the mention of that other woman's name, cried out when Chase's defenses were lowered.

Kate was pretty sure by the stiffness of Chase's body that he knew what he'd said. Perhaps he was even now trying to concoct some excuse, some reason for why he had his cock in her, and another woman's name on his lips.

Kate shifted and shrugged beneath Chase, indicating with her body for him to roll off her. He did, falling beside her onto his back. The other woman, the woman obviously still in his heart, lay between them, as intrusive as if she'd been flesh and blood.

Kate waited for the rush of apologies, the explanations, the excuses, but Chase remained silent. She shifted onto her side and lifted herself on one elbow, resting her cheek in her hand. She peered at Chase, who was staring at the ceiling, his expression unreadable.

Should she call him on it, or just let it go? So, he was still hung up on another woman. He was *with* her. And damn it, she wanted him. The scene in the bondage room had been *amazing*. It went beyond anything she'd ever experienced. It went beyond anything she'd imagined. It had been the most intense, thrilling experience of her life. Then, when he'd taken her to his bed and so sweetly but confidently undressed her, his blue eyes looking straight into her heart, she'd sensed his sexual mastery and realized she'd found a real man at last.

The way he'd touched her, with such intimate sureness, showed her he was not only comfortable around a woman's body, but *loved* women. It was clear from how he'd made love to her with his mouth and hands, and finally his cock, that he didn't regard her as a means to his own ends, as she'd found with so many men, whose primary focus and goal was to get laid, no matter what or how. And when he'd held her wrists against the mattress, it was perfect, it was just what she needed, that added dash of erotic thrill.

She should just let his gaffe pass, keep quiet, pretend she hadn't noticed. Instead, she found herself asking, "What just happened?"

Chase turned his head slowly toward her, his eyes dark and filled with grief. "I'm so sorry, Kate."

Kate's blood ran cold. Was he dismissing her? She waited, her heart beating unpleasantly fast against her ribs. Forcing herself to stay calm, Kate said, "You want to tell me what's going on? Is this Lisa person still in the picture?"

Chase pulled himself upright and turned to face her. "I thought I was over her, Kate." Kate felt her heart fall down into her stomach. Her hands had curled into fists, the nails cutting into her palms. She tensed, waiting to hear what he had to say.

"Lisa committed suicide a year ago last May. I should have told you sooner. I wanted to, but the timing just never seemed right. You're the first woman I've been with since Lisa. The first person I've made love to. I thought I was ready to move on." He sighed heavily. "Man, I'm sorry. I've really fucked things up, huh?"

Kate stared at him, stunned. "Suicide," she whispered. "I just thought she'd broken up with you. I had no idea…" She trailed off, compassion mingled with relief flooding her senses. She knew it was selfish, and it wasn't that she was glad the poor woman was dead, but at least Chase wasn't still actively in love with her.

Was he?

She reached for Chase, putting a hand on his arm. He didn't respond and after a moment she let it fall away. Something had changed in him. It was as if he had slipped away from her. His face was closed, the sparkle gone from his eyes.

The room suddenly felt cold. Kate hugged herself, aware of her nakedness. She saw her blouse crumpled on the floor at the foot of the bed. Scooting down, she reached for it and pulled it protectively around her shoulders.

~*~

Chase felt as if he'd fallen into a bad dream. He couldn't form the right words to make everything better again. He didn't know what to say. He'd honestly thought he'd finally cast off the shroud of grief he'd been wearing like a second skin for so long. He'd believed he was ready to move on at last.

Yet now the past was coming between him and the best thing to happen to him in years — maybe ever. Yet now he could feel Lisa's dark spirit hovering in the room, looming between them, insinuating herself into his life again, just when he'd thought he could finally let her go once and for all.

He stared helplessly at Kate, wishing he could undo what had been done, take back what had been said. He could see by the hurt in her face that it was too late.

Chase felt himself sinking back into a dark, all too familiar space. The black, boney fingers of depression that had gripped him the first several months after Lisa's death were reaching for him. He closed his eyes, giving in to the pull. Maybe he'd been fooling himself all this time. Maybe Lisa and he were cut from the same dark cloth. Kate didn't deserve to be saddled with his issues. Better just to go back into himself, into his safe, quiet world of rope and fantasy.

He realized Kate was watching him. "Are you going to talk to me, Chase? I feel like you've, I don't know, left the room somehow. What's going on?" She was hugging herself protectively, rocking slightly like a child comforting herself. It wasn't love he saw in her face, but pity.

It was that expression of pity that pushed him the rest of the way down. In the space of a few minutes, Kate had gone from eager, adoring new lover to just another person who felt sorry for poor Chase. He could hardly bear the transformation. He turned his head away.

"Chase. Do you want me to go?" Kate's voice was small and sad.

"Maybe it would be best," he managed, his voice strangled in his throat. He could hear her moving about the room as she dressed and collected her things. He turned back in time to see her walking out the door. His heart sank like a stone.

Chapter 13

Kate sighed and pushed back from the keyboard, abandoning even the pretense of working any longer. Chase Saunders was eighty miles away, but he might as well have been in the room.

She'd been numb on the drive back from his place, stunned and confused by what had happened. It was as if Chase had changed into a different person before her eyes. The confident, sexy man who had taken control of her body and soul had seemed to evaporate, leaving behind a broken, miserable shell of a man.

Maybe it would be best.

Best for whom? Why had she capitulated so easily? Why hadn't she tried to get him to open up more — to confide in her? To trust her as she'd trusted him? She'd felt so connected to him during the experience in the bondage room and afterwards, making love. He had unlocked feelings she'd known were there, but had never been able to tap. She understood on a visceral level now how powerful the blending of pleasure and erotic pain could be, the silken tug of the rope, the shivery ache of desire when a dominant man claimed what was his.

How could he give her that joy one moment and then take it all away the next? Was he still in love with a ghost? Should Kate just quietly accept his sad decree that it was best she go? Forget the amazing afternoon they'd shared?

He'd assured her he was over Lisa, and yet he'd sent her away. The way he'd acted, closing in on himself, shutting her out—how could she reconcile that with the way he'd made love to her? With the way he'd looked into her eyes?

She could almost feel his strong arms wrapping around her, pulling her into an embrace as he kissed her. She massaged her wrists, which ached for the snug wrap of soft rope that had bound her, arms high overhead, to a silver ring.

"I want that," she said aloud. "I want what he offered." And more than that, more than just the taste of D/s he'd given her, she wanted him to make love to her again. She wanted to feel his heavy, comforting weight atop her, as his cock hard swiveled and thrust inside her, sending spirals of rapturous pleasure that radiated from her sex and filled her entire being. The experience in the bondage room had heightened their lovemaking afterward, lifting it to something magical and sublime. She'd been completely pulled out of herself, released in a way she'd never experienced before and longed to experience again.

Kate looked at the clock. It was nearly midnight. What was Chase doing now? Had he gone to sleep? How had he spent the rest of the afternoon and evening? He'd looked so woebegone when she'd left.

She thought about how degraded and terrified she'd felt at the play party when John Brighton had taken her too far, too fast, and how Chase had suddenly appeared. He'd uncuffed her, helped her dress, said soothing, kind things to her and never once, not during or later, told her what a fool she had been, or that he'd told her so. He'd offered unstinting support and understanding every step of the way. He'd been gracious and kind in the face of her humiliation and confusion.

He'd reached out to her. Surely she owed him the same? Maybe he wasn't ready for a new lover, but a person could always use a friend.

Kate saved the manuscript she was working on and shut down her computer. She left the small study, flicking off the light. Grabbing her purse and keys, she walked out the door, a woman on a mission.

~*~

Chase heard the sound of the door knocker but didn't process it at first. He'd been dozing on and off for the last several hours, jerked awake repeatedly by vague, menacing nightmares he refused to examine.

After Kate had left, he'd lain in the bed, naked and alone. It had felt as if someone had placed a heavy lead blanket over him. It kept him pinned there for a long time, too paralyzed with misery to move. It was as if, when Kate left, she took all the light and air from the place with her, leaving him in a vacuum, more alone than ever before.

Kate was the first person he'd told about Lisa's death since it had happened. Of course others knew — her family and his, their friends at the time, the few there were. But he'd never come out and said it aloud to another person.

Thoughts he hadn't permitted himself since before her death had suddenly come flooding back into his brain. Thoughts he'd banished as disloyal to her memory, but which would no longer be contained.

Lisa had often and effusively told him she loved him. She adored him. She lived for him. He was her life. She needed him, she would say, in a way that was beyond speech, beyond time. At first he'd been delighted, thinking he'd finally found someone who truly loved him. But when her illness would show its twisted, dark head, when she stopped taking her medication, insisting it made her feel detached and empty, instead of passionate, he sensed there was something not quite right about her protestations of undying love.

Toward the end of her life, the end of their relationship, which probably would have ended even if she'd hadn't taken such a final way out, he'd come to realize what she'd felt for him wasn't love. It was need and habit, an addiction. He was the object of her obsession, but he had never been real to her. Nothing, it turned out, was real to her except her continued and abiding psychic pain.

The knocker sounded again and Chase looked at the clock beside his bed. It was nearly two in the morning. He stumbled from the bed, grabbing a pair of cotton drawstring pants from the dresser as he went and pulling them on.

"Coming," he called. He pulled open the door, expecting to see his elderly neighbor, Mr. Hicks, who sometimes got confused about what day or time it was, and asked for a lift to the post office or the barbershop at odd hours.

Kate stood there, her face pale, her eyes glittering in the moonlight. Chase stepped back, his heart surging, not daring to make any assumptions. "Kate, it's you." The boney fingers eased their grip on his heart.

"Can I come in?"

"Yes, of course." He stepped back and gestured for her to enter. Kate stepped into the foyer and he closed the door.

"I'm sorry," she said with a small, shy smile. "I know you were probably asleep. I would have called, but I didn't want you to say not to come."

Wordlessly, Chase held out his arms, relief and fledgling joy flooding through his body as Kate moved into his embrace. They stood that way a long time. Chase felt as if Kate were sweeping away his darkness with her light. She clung to him, murmuring his name. This didn't feel like a pity hug. Could it be she was back not because she felt sorry for him, but because she wanted to be there, with him?

Finally Chase pulled gently from her embrace. "I was an idiot to let you go. I'm sorry, Kate. I guess there are some things I haven't dealt with yet, regarding Lisa. I'm glad you came back."

He led Kate to the loveseat and they sat down. Kate turned to him, her expression serious. "I shouldn't have let you send me away. It was clear you were hurting. I kept thinking after I left of how you'd been there for me after that scene with John Brighton. How you not only stepped in as my knight in shining armor, but reached out with that email. You didn't even know me, but you made it clear you were there for me. You were a friend from the beginning."

She put her hand on his leg and he covered it with his own. "Even if you aren't ready, Chase. Ready for something new with me..." She paused and swallowed. She smiled, though tears had suddenly appeared in her eyes. "I want you to know I'm your friend. I'm here for you. You can talk to me. You can trust me."

"Thank you, Kate." Chase reached for Kate, enfolding her in his arms. "That means more to me than you can imagine. I've shut myself off from the world for too long. You reawakened something in me, something I thought had died. I appreciate your offer of friendship very much." He stroked her hair. "I honestly hadn't realized how isolated I had become, how closed off from my feelings." He let her go and sat back, shaking his head. "I like to think I'm so together. That I can handle anything. That I don't need anyone. And for this past year, I've managed to make that work, at least on the surface. But the truth is, there's a lot of stuff I haven't really dealt with. I thought I was doing okay, but really I was in denial."

He turned to face her, stroking her soft cheek. She leaned into his hand and his heart ached with longing. She was giving him a second chance. *Jesus, Saunders, don't blow it. Not again.* He took a breath and continued. "Finding you—making love to you today—it was like opening a raw wound. I want to heal, Kate. I want to let go of the past, of her."

"How did it happen?" Kate asked gently. "How did she do it?"

Chase didn't answer right away. "Are you sure you want to talk about this?"

"Only if you're okay with it," Kate replied. "It might actually be good for you to say it out loud. I get the sense you've been keeping a lot in for a long time."

"Yeah. You can say that again." Chase hesitated and then finally said, "She...she slit her wrists. I found her in her bathtub. I still have nightmares about it."

"Oh, Chase, that's horrible."

"It was pretty awful." Chase didn't want to burden Kate with the images that were indelibly branded into his own mind, and so he didn't elaborate. When he'd come over that evening to Lisa's place, he'd discovered her body in the bathtub. She lay white as death in a pool of red water, her wrists slit with one of the utility knives he used in his workshop. It had been found in the tub when they'd drained it. An empty bottle of vodka lay on its side on the bath mat.

"To make matters worse, I must have passed out right after I made the call to 911. When the cops got there, I was all covered in blood—my own, of course, but they didn't know that for sure." He paused, feeling as if his throat were closing. It took him a moment to figure out the hot pressure behind his eyes was tears he'd never allowed himself to spill. He swallowed and blinked, forcing himself to go on. "I'd hit my head on the corner of the countertop on my way to the floor. I was pretty much in shock, and wasn't very coherent when the police were questioning me.

"I was actually a suspect for a while, and Lisa's family didn't help matters. They told the police about what they referred to as Lisa's perverted lifestyle. They got a warrant to search my place. It was pretty scary for a while, on top of the horror of what she'd done."

Kate touched Chase's shoulder and stroked his arm, her voice tender. "It must have been so hard for you. I can't even imagine." Chase felt raw and vulnerable. He'd buried the sorrow and helpless rage of that time behind a wall of self-control. At her soft touch he felt the wall crumbling.

He couldn't stop the tears that were welling from his eyes, rolling hot and fast down his cheeks. "Jesus." His voice cracked. "I'm sorry. I don't want to do this..." He hid his face in his hands.

"It's okay," Kate whispered, stroking his hair. "You're allowed to cry. It's healing."

The last bricks of the internal wall crumbled to dust in the face of her gentle kindness. Chase gave in to the onslaught of his sorrow, unable to regain control. Kate wrapped her arms around his shaking shoulders. He was barely able to catch his breath as the sobs wracked his body.

He cried for Lisa.

He cried for the life he'd lived, never quite managing to get it right. He cried for the past year, spent in lonely, quiet desperation, clinging to a semblance of normalcy, when inside he'd blamed himself for Lisa's death. If only he could have done more, done something...

Kate held him, rocking him gently. He cried until there was nothing left. He felt lightheaded and completely drained. Pulling away from Kate's gentle embrace, he let his head fall back against the loveseat.

"Where are tissues? I'll get you some," Kate said.

"In the kitchen," Chase said, somehow surprised that his voice box functioned. He wouldn't have been surprised if all that sobbing had sucked the very sound out of him for good. He couldn't remember the last time he'd cried like that, if ever. He'd shed tears at Lisa's funeral, but they'd been quiet, contained tears, nothing like this red-faced, heaving splatter of emotion he'd forced Kate to witness.

She returned with the box of tissues and Chase gratefully grabbed a handful, wiping his face and blowing his nose. "Man, I'm sorry," he began.

Kate stopped him with a finger on his lips. "No. Enough being sorry. For both of us. You and I apologize way too much. I'm noticing that. You've been through hell and back, that much is obvious. If you don't mind me crashing here, how about let's go to bed. I haven't been to sleep yet and I bet you're wiped out. I know I'm always exhausted after a really good cry."

Chase smiled and realized she was right. It had been a really *good* cry. He'd always regarded crying as a sign of weakness, at least in a man, as something to be avoided at all costs. But he felt, well, not good precisely, but relieved. The stranglehold of guilt and remorse that had been suffocating him without his conscious knowledge had been loosened with that one good cry.

He wasn't naïve enough to think he was done now — all better and Lisa completely behind him — but at least it was a start. It was something. And Kate had been there to witness it. To help him through it.

"Thank you," he said.

"For what?"

"For being there."

~*~

They were snuggled together in the bed, Kate on her side, Chase behind her, his arms around her. Chase had lent Kate a T-shirt to sleep in. They'd shared a midnight snack of cereal with banana before going to bed. They hadn't said much while they ate, but the silence was companionable, not strained. Kate was so glad she'd come back, and even though it was going on three in the morning, she could have stayed up longer to let Chase talk, if he'd wanted to.

But looking at him, she could see he was dead on his feet, his eyes red-rimmed from crying and fatigue. A good night's sleep could do wonders, especially after a good cry. She sensed Chase didn't cry often, and that in doing so in front of her, he'd shared something even more intimate than sex.

She nestled back against him, thinking she wouldn't mind a repeat of their lovemaking earlier that day, well, technically yesterday, but gave herself a silent scolding. The poor man was exhausted. Let him sleep. She closed her eyes and let herself drift, surprised how relaxed and content she was. Usually she tossed and turned when in a strange bed, unable to get comfortable.

Chase's breathing was coming slow and even, with an occasional soft snore. Could she sleep with someone beside her? She'd grown quite used to her solitude over the past two years. Even though it was late and she knew she should be wiped out, she doubted she...

When Kate next opened her eyes, the room was filled with the pink light of early dawn. Chase was asleep beside her on his back, one arm slung over his face. The sheet had slipped down, exposing his chest. On an impulse, Kate leaned over and lightly kissed his left nipple, circling it with her tongue. He stirred but didn't open his eyes.

She kissed his other nipple and then trailed her tongue down his body, as he'd done the day before to her. "Mmmm," Chase murmured, though he still didn't move. Emboldened, Kate pushed back the sheets and tugged at the string on Chase's pants, slipping her hand inside the waistband.

He was naked beneath, his cock nestled in its bed of pubic curls. She wrapped her fingers around his cock and stroked it, enjoying the sensation of silky, warm skin covering his rapidly hardening shaft.

"Mmmm," Chase said again, and she could tell he was fully awake now. She glanced at his face. His eyes were still hidden by his arm, his lips softly parted. Kate released his cock long enough to pull down the loose cotton pants to his thighs. She examined his cock and balls, something she hadn't had a chance to do properly the day before.

His cock was thick and straight, the balls full and lush beneath it. Scooting down on her side, Kate leaned over him and licked along the fat vein that ran its length, feeling the pulsing heat beneath her tongue. Chase moaned. Kate closed her lips over the head of his shaft, sucking at the drop of clear, sweet pre-cum at its tip.

She cupped his balls in one hand and lowered her head completely over his cock, milking it with her lips and tongue until the head was touching the back of her throat. Chase groaned and she felt his hand rest lightly on top of her head.

Kate felt her power as a woman and a sexual being. She loved pleasing a man in this way, not only for his pleasure, but for her own, thrilling each time that she could make a man come, make him moan and beg, make him cry out in ecstasy.

She began to suck in earnest, stroking his balls with one hand, using the other to grip the base of his shaft. The hand on her head pushed harder, forcing her down onto his shaft and, because she hadn't been expecting it, making her gag. When she tried to push back against it, he held her fast.

This subtle shift in power between them sent something shooting through Kate's veins like a thousand jolts of electricity. She felt the ache in her pussy, a yearning to feel his power, his control. He was controlling her very breath with his cock, and the firm hand on her head.

When he let her go she reared back, gasping for air. He let her catch her breath and then the hand was returned, pushing down steadily, forcing his way down her throat, though she was a most willing participant.

She reveled in what he was doing, thrilled in a way she never imagined. She'd explored the obvious BDSM avenues of light bondage, spanking and flogging, but no one had ever exerted this kind of overt, sensual control.

Kate became totally absorbed in the erotic interplay of pleasuring Chase, while simultaneously being controlled by him. Each time he held her down a few seconds longer, testing her ability to hold her breath, or more to the point, to obey him. She knew she was completely safe with Chase. Because the foundation of trust was there, it left her free to fully experience the thrill of breath play.

Chase began to moan again, thrusting up to meet her mouth, forcing his cock deep into her throat. With his hand still on her head, she was unable to resist him, but she didn't want to. She worked her throat and tongue, massaging him as best she could while impaled on the thick, hard shaft. Her pussy was throbbing.

"Kate, yes, oh god, Kate," he cried. She could feel him climaxing. He released her head as he did, stiffening and shuddering as long streams of semen shot down her throat, too far back for her to even need to swallow.

He sagged back against the mattress and Kate slowly lifted herself from his shiny cock. Chase raised his head and looked at her through half-closed eyes. "*That* was incredible," he asserted with such sincerity that Kate laughed. She was pleased not only with herself, but with him. After all, this time he'd remembered her name.

Chapter 14

Kate couldn't stop smiling as she drove back toward the country late that afternoon. She hadn't been looking for a man when she'd signed up for the BDSM weekend. She'd been looking for an experience. Something she could write about.

She hadn't expected to meet someone like Chase. In fact, she hadn't known someone like Chase existed. He was a poet, not only in word but in action. He took the excitement and intensity of BDSM, but shaped it into something altogether new. He lifted the experience from the merely erotic to something spiritual.

That very idea seemed contrary to Kate's prior notion of BDSM, which, she now realized, she had viewed as exciting and daring, but certainly not sublime. She was aching to experience again that transcendent state of being he'd lifted her to during the flogging. When he'd talked in theory before about the power of erotic submission, she hadn't really understood. Even now, she recognized they had barely scratched the surface. They'd shared one scene and made love twice. Not exactly a long term relationship. Yet she felt closer to this man than she'd ever felt to the other men she'd been with. Maybe it was because of how he'd shared his grief and his tears with her. It had brought them closer more quickly than just the lovemaking alone would have.

They'd made plans to see each other again tomorrow. She'd wanted to stay at his place, reveling in the thrill and excitement of someone new. But at the same time she needed to go back home. When she'd made the decision to drive down to Queens, she had left so suddenly in the middle of the night, bringing none of her things with her, no makeup, no fresh clothes, nothing. She'd showered at his place, but had had to step back into her old clothes.

Not to mention, she was exhausted. She hadn't fallen asleep until sometime after three that morning, and over the course of the next twelve hours she'd had maybe five hours total sleep, not in a row. It would be good to crash. She would go to bed early and awaken at dawn to write a chapter before their scheduled lunch date at Maude's.

When Kate arrived the next day at the café, Chase was already sitting at a table in the corner with two glasses of peach iced tea on the table. He waved and smiled, and Kate's heart did a little flip flop. It occurred to her she was falling in love. She shook away the idea — it was way too soon, she admonished herself, way too soon.

They ordered sandwiches from the same waitress, who remembered them and greeted them warmly. They talked of easy things at first — the novel Kate was working on, Chase's rope business, the benefits of country versus city living.

Carefully, she brought the conversation around to something more personal. "Does it feel strange to be with someone new? After all this time?"

"It feels wonderful," Chase said warmly. "You know, I learned something yesterday. I've spent the past year grieving for a lost love that had really died well before Lisa did. I know that sounds harsh, but I've been thinking a lot about it. Lisa was a good person, don't get me wrong. But the thing that was broken in her, the twist in her spirit, the flaw in her biochemical makeup, however you want to characterize it, had been there long before I met her. She did take medication for a bipolar disorder, but only when she felt like it. She said it made her feel bland, like the life had been sucked out of her. She felt more alive, she said, when she was careening from the highs to the lows. It was both exhilarating and exhausting to be around her.

"I was in love with her at first. She was exotic and unusual. She was wildly creative and sometimes very dark. Back then I confused the mental illness as something romantic—she was the wild streak that offset my rather careful, plodding personality."

"Oh, not at all—" Kate began to protest, but Chase stopped her with a raised hand.

He smiled. "I'm not putting myself down. It was more a matter of contrast, you see. I was quiet, stable, slow to speak. She was wild, tumultuous, at turns lavishing me with attention or totally withdrawing. Life with Lisa was never boring." He gave a rueful laugh but the smile fell away as he continued. "I thought I could save her," he said quietly. "I thought I, and I alone, through D/s and through unconditional love, could repair the damage inside her. I think I had stopped loving her well before she killed herself, and well before she accused me of that very thing."

"She said that? That you didn't love her?"

Chase nodded. "She did. She even told me in advance she was going to kill herself. She said I no longer loved her, and therefore her life no longer had meaning, and so she was going to end it. This was several weeks before she actually did it. At the time I shook it off as more of her dramatics, and in fact it just made me angry. I denied her assertion, of course and reassured her of my love, but she was right. I didn't love her. In fact I resented the shit out of her, but I held those feelings down. I denied them to myself because she *needed* me. I could save her if I just did X or Y or Z well enough. And then she would be happy.

"But it was never enough. I didn't understand then that it could never be enough. I couldn't save her." His voice cracked and Kate felt tears welling in her eyes.

"We can never save someone else," she said softly. She reached across the table and put her hand over his. "We can't be responsible for someone else's happiness."

"I know." Chase nodded. "I understand that now." He put his other hand over hers and smiled. "Sorry for dumping all that on you. I'm telling you because I want you to understand that I've had a kind of epiphany. Since meeting you, it's like a six ton weight has been lifted from my shoulders. I feel so...light. Yes, that's the word. I was carrying so much darkness for so long, I forgot what it felt like to be happy.

"I can only imagine you're a little nervous about this past relationship, and how it's going to color whatever develops between us going forward. I'm not going to lie and say I'm completely over what happened, or that I'll never think of her again. What happened is a part of my life experience now, but it's not the defining experience.

"What I'm trying to say is, I'm ready now, truly ready, to move forward. I refuse to let the past keep me tethered to something that was never really right for me in the first place. I'm ready, Kate, to take on the world. I know this sounds corny, but I'm ready to live again."

He laughed and slapped his forehead, a slight flush of embarrassment creeping over his cheeks. "Man, would you listen to me go on? I don't think I've talked this much in a whole *year*, much less all at once. Tell me to shut up, will you?"

Kate laughed too. "You have a lot to say. I'm glad you trust me enough to say it to *me*. I'm honored, actually." And she meant it. In the brief time they'd known each other, she'd sensed Chase was reserved, not in the sense of holding back, but he was a man who took his time. Who thought before blurting out whatever was on his mind (unlike her, she thought with chagrin, who all too often spoke first and thought later). This long speech, this intimate baring of what had to be the most difficult thing he had ever faced, moved Kate. It made her feel closer to him. It made her want to know him better.

She found she wanted to give him something back. To share something held close within herself as a reciprocal show of trust. And so she said, "I've been thinking a lot too. About the whole D/s thing. Where it fits into my life—if it fits in. I mean, I've always been secretly fascinated with what I looked at as the dark, dangerous world of BDSM, but I never went out looking for it. I tried some with my ex-boyfriend, but we were really just playing around. It got me to wondering, maybe I'm just dabbling right now. You know, trying out something new, and it's going to get old after a while, just like anything else. Fizzle out. Lose the thrill."

"Do you believe that?" Chase looked into her eyes and Kate found herself captivated by his stare. "I don't, Kate. I think you are a born submissive. I think it's a part of who you are. You haven't had a lot of experience yet, but that doesn't make who and what you are any less real."

Kate pulled away from his gaze and looked down at her lap. A part of her resisted this idea, and she tried to voice her confusion. "If that's true, why did I wait until I was twenty-nine years old to even bring up my fantasies to someone else? If it's this basic part of me, as you say, how did I live my whole life without it?"

"I can't speak for you, Kate, but I'd venture to guess you've felt something missing, something lacking in both yourself and whoever you've been with, as a result. I'm guessing you always felt cheated, but never really understood why."

He leaned forward, his voice taking on a low, sensual timbre that made Kate press her thighs together to ease the sudden ache between her legs. "You know what you are, Kate, when you quiet the voices in your head, when you close your eyes and just *feel* what is right for you. I watched you, I felt the connection when you flew. That wasn't dabbling, Kate. That was you embracing a basic, intrinsic part of your being. It's not only what you want. It's what you *need*."

Kate sighed, the long, lingering sound of it escaping before she knew she'd made a sound. Chase tilted his head and narrowed his eyes. "I have an idea," he said. "Is there a hardware store near here?"

"Yeah, just down the street. Why?"

"I want to conduct a little experiment." Chase paid the bill, refusing Kate's effort to contribute. He also left a sizable tip for the waitress, Kate noted with satisfaction, aware he'd just passed yet another of her unspoken tests for a suitable partner, and laughing at herself for even noticing.

They left Chase's car in the café parking lot and drove together to Tom's Hardware. Once inside, Kate followed Chase along the narrow, crowded aisles, intrigued with what he was up to. He stopped in front of the spools of chain link. Turning to her, he said, "Pick one. A nice solid one."

"What for?" Kate asked.

"For you. To wear around your neck."

"Oh." Kate felt the heat creeping up her throat and cheeks. She couldn't deny the sudden ache deep in her loins. Her nipples were perking against her tank top and she wrapped her arms across her chest to hide them.

"Go on," Chase said. "Pick one."

Kate examined the spools of chain in front of her and touched one with thick oval links, nervously biting her lip as she did so. Chase unraveled a length, looked at her and back at the chain, measuring with his fingers. Using the chain cutter hanging from a hook nearby, he cut the chain and held up the length for Kate to see.

Right there in the aisle, he draped the heavy metal around her neck, using his hand to hold it closed at her throat. Kate gasped, her heart suddenly beating wildly, a tremor of lust and something else, something primal and urgent, moving through her frame.

"You see," Chase said softly, a triumphant gleam in his eye. "Embrace it. It's time to learn who you really are. If you trust me, we'll learn together."

~*~

Chase traced the curve of Kate's jaw, moving his fingers along her throat, touching the cold, heavy chain resting over her delicate collarbone. They were in Kate's bedroom, a wide, airy space with pale green walls and white ceiling and trim, a large white ceiling fan whirring lazily overheard. Lovely Kate was naked and bound in his silken ropes on the bed.

He'd bought the chain and a padlock to go with it, and had Kate carry it in her hands out to the car. Her reaction when he'd placed it on her neck had thrilled him, though it had come as no surprise. She was, like him, born to this. It came as naturally as breathing. She was the yin to his yang, the pair of them forming a perfect circle of give and take, of dominance and submission, perhaps one day of love.

She looked so beautiful lying there on her back, her wrists bound to her ankles, legs spread wide to reveal her sex, the petals engorged with desire and glistening with need. Her hair was wild about her face, her green eyes wide as she watched him remove the flogger from his duffel bag. He'd briefly considered the cane when he'd thrown a few items for play into his bag that morning but decided against it, given Kate's recent traumatic experience.

Chase's balls were aching, his cock rigid in the confines of his jeans. He had taken off his shirt and sandals, but had kept his pants on while he bound the beautiful girl with artful Shibari knots and positioned her just so on the bed.

He began by stroking Kate's flesh with the soft suede tresses, dragging it over her breasts and flat stomach, teasing it along her pussy, stroking her thighs with it. Kate closed her eyes and sighed, the sound sensual and throaty.

Gauging she was ready, he began to flog her lightly at first, slowly increasing the intensity and the tempo. He saw she was holding her breath, her muscles tensing in anticipation of the strokes. "Breathe," he told her. "Let go of the tension. Flow with the pain. Move through it to get where you need to be."

She drew a shallow breath, and another. "That's it," he encouraged, trying not to focus on his raging erection, and his longing to plunge into her. This was for her—he would take his time, and he knew it would make it all the more powerful when at last he claimed her body with his. "Nice and slow. Yes. Stay focused on your breathing. Good."

He began again, covering her body from thigh to chest, slapping the leather against her skin, watching it turn pink. He let the tresses land on her breasts, catching the erect nipples. Kate yelped and jerked in her restraints. "Breathe," Chase reminded her, his cock nearly bursting.

Kate drew a shuddery breath. Chase stroked her cheek with his hand and leaned down to kiss her lips. "You're doing great," he said. "Shall we continue?"

"Yes, please," she whispered, and he smiled.

He complied, again warming the skin, harder this time, adding the sting he knew she needed to fly. She began to jerk against her bonds again, her chest heaving.

He angled himself to strike the tender folds of her bared sex, though much more gently, of course. Kate's eyes flew open and she yelped. He didn't stop, aware she needed him to continue, even if she was frightened or nervous. He focused on her pussy, whipping it with the just the tips of the strands, keeping time with her breathing.

"No, no, I can't—" she finally said, when an especially stinging blow found its mark.

"You can," Chase assured her. "You are." He moved the whip, however, focusing again on her thighs and breasts, turning the creamy skin a rosy red while Kate panted and writhed beneath the leather kiss.

When he could stand it no longer, he dropped the flogger and pulled off his clothes, slipping on a condom with lightning speed before climbing over the bound woman. "Jesus, I want you, Kate," he said urgently. He had meant to untie her before he made love to her, but his need was too great. For too long his heart had been open only to bitterness and regret. Now the passion, which he'd buried for so long, was once again wild in his heart.

His mouth was on hers, his weight supported on his arms as he eased into her. Her cunt actually drew him in, its muscles clenching and pulling him deeper as she arched up as best she could in her restrained position. He made love to her with a ferocity that surprised him, that caused rivulets of sweat to run down his back and chest. He wanted to be gentle, but lust had made him a wild man.

They became pure movement, raw desire, moving together in the timeless rhythm of lovers. Kate began to mew, soft sweet urgent sounds that fired Chase's blood. He heard her soft moan of pleasure as her pussy spasmed and her body heated like a flame beneath him. He let himself go then, surging with her into orgasm, his weight fully on her now, crushing her beneath him.

When he could catch his breath, Chase forced himself to move, rolling from Kate, whose head was to the side, eyes closed. He quickly undid the knots and pulled the ropes from her body. Gently he straightened her legs, stroking the flesh, massaging the muscles in her calves. She lay limp with eyes still closed, but she was smiling, catlike and content.

Chase gathered her into his arms and held her, smoothing the wild hair back from her forehead. "I love you," he wanted to whisper, but held himself back from saying it. He would know when the time was right. For now, they were still too new. Instead he kissed her gently.

Kate opened her eyes and said a single word, managing to infuse it with tenderness and awe. "You," she said.

"Us," he replied.

Chapter 15

Kate finally reconnected with Stacey in mid July, meeting her in the city at the hair salon where Stacey worked. After giving Kate the grand tour, Stacey took her to an Indian dive nearby. Over spicy curry and mango milk shakes, Kate opened up enough to admit what she'd only hinted at about the scene with John Brighton in their email exchanges to that point.

Embarrassed, she faltered over the words, but Stacey understood enough to express her outrage. "That prick should have his balls cut off," she announced in a loud voice, causing more than one head to turn in the small restaurant. "At the very least, you need to send a formal complaint to Power Play, letting them know he ignored your safeword and refused to end the scene when you wanted it over. No way they'll want to keep someone like that on their payroll. Especially not after *I* spread the word."

"You're right," Kate said. Enough time had passed for the humiliation she'd felt that night to ease its sting. Chase had taught her a new way, a romantic way to experience erotic submission. She understood now she had done nothing wrong and had nothing to be ashamed of. She would expose John Brighton for the bully he was.

"Enough about that," Stacey said, rubbing her hands together. "Tell me about Chase. The juicy stuff you left out of your emails. I think it's so great you two are together. It's a lot more fun to actually live it than just to write about it, am I right?"

Kate smiled. "Oh, yeah. I've been curious all my life, but I had no idea of the power of this kind of relationship. He's ruined me for anything vanilla, I can tell you that."

"I'm with you on that one," Stacey enthused. "Give me a man with a whip in his hand over a bouquet of flowers any day."

"How about both?" Kate rejoined, thinking of the flowers Chase gave her all the time from his garden. She tried to put her new feelings into words for Stacey. "It's like I'm more alive, somehow. More *me*. I feel different inside, though it's hard to explain just how." She pondered. "Maybe it's more of what I'm *not* anymore. I don't have to hold onto fronts and covers that protect me from anyone really touching me, touching my heart, my...soul..."

She waited for Stacey to make fun of her lofty words, but Stacey nodded solemnly and then smiled. "You're in love," she asserted. "But I'm guessing you haven't said the L word to each other yet, have you?"

"No," Kate admitted. "Though it's been edging its way into my mind, I will admit. Maybe I'm waiting for him to say it first."

"Tell him, Kate. Let him know what's in your heart."

"What if he doesn't say it back?"

Stacey shrugged. "What's life without risk? Anyway, just because he doesn't say it, doesn't mean he doesn't think it. Men are funny like that sometimes."

That night Kate was restless, anxious about a writing deadline and mulling over plotlines in her head. She was flopping around the bed like a fish on the deck of a boat and apologized when she woke Chase.

He gathered her into his arms and stroked her hair. He began to sing, softly, in a sweet tenor. She'd recognized the song, a lullaby called *All Through the Night*.

Sleep, my child, let peace attend thee

All through the night

Guardian angels God will send thee

All through the night...

She nestled against him, ridiculously happy, and the words tumbled from her lips. "Oh, Chase, I love you."

"I love you," he'd answered at once. "More than you can imagine."

The love they shared was part of the difference she felt inside herself, but it was more than that. Much more. She had a new kind of confidence and serenity. She felt more...herself. Actualized, real, solid, serene. She'd tried to share these new feelings with Chase, to put them into words.

He'd understood. "It's because you're finally *being* yourself. You're finally tapping into that essence of submission that was kept dormant for so long. You are, though it sounds strange to say, finally being *you*, all of you, not just pieces strung together to give a semblance of a total person."

It made sense. And it had advantages other than just a new sense of sexual contentment and confidence. Her writing had changed. Her editors had noticed and commented on a new maturity and a more complex passion. She wrote constantly now, that is, when she wasn't bound in Chase's playroom, or stretched naked on his bed, or nestled sweetly in his arms. She'd finished the novel about the widowed farm girl and her lover, and was brimming with ideas for her next projects.

Chase was busy too, his online rope making business really taking off. He'd found a small factory space to rent and hired two additional workers to meet the burgeoning demand for his soft, supple rope and how-to videos on the art of sensual bondage.

This morning, however, neither was working. They'd both promised to take the day off and focus exclusively on each other, which suited Kate fine. She was in the shower, doing something she hoped would please Chase.

He had often talked of a sub's duty to withhold nothing from her Dom. When she gave herself to him, in that supreme act of trust, it had to be complete—nothing held back—if she were sincere in her desire to submit.

Kate wanted to do that, and did try her best. She didn't cover her body, or deny Chase when he asked something of her that made her nervous or embarrassed. They would talk it through—he encouraged and even insisted that she tell him any time she was uncomfortable with something he was asking, and they would work through it together.

That day he was going to introduce her to the cane. Properly, he said, not the way she'd experienced it before. They rarely referred to John Brighton but the memory of that night still had the power to unsettle Kate. And the thought of the cane frightened her.

Chase understood this fear, but said, "You're ready now, Kate. You've proven you can handle a great deal as a sub, with grace and focus. We've taken our time as we move to each new level together. To continue to deny you the cane is to let him steal something from us. We won't allow that man's stupidity and mishandling of a scene to be a defining limit in our relationship. We won't give him that power."

Kate dried off and walked into the bedroom, dropping her towel as she stood in front of Chase, who was lying naked on the sheets. He looked at her, his eyebrows lifting. "Kate, you did that for me?"

She nodded, biting her lower lip, forcing herself to stand proud. He reached for her and she stepped closer. He drew his fingers over her smooth, shaven skin and smiled. "Nice," he said. "Very, very nice."

"It's symbolic," she offered. "I wanted to show you I withhold nothing. That I am fully bared for you, Sir."

She had lately taken to calling him Sir when she was in a submissive mindset, and he hadn't seemed to mind. Indeed, he seemed to like it. It felt natural, especially when thanking him for an especially intense bondage scene or sensual whipping.

"Thank you, Sir," she would breathe.

"You're welcome, sweet sub girl," he would reply.

Chase's hand was still on her mons. "Spread your legs," he commanded, and she obeyed.

He slipped his fingers into the cleft of her sex, stroking her, immediately arousing her. "Are you ready for the cane, sub girl?"

"Yes, Sir," she whispered, hoping this was true.

After breakfast they went into his bondage room. Chase had moved the portable suspension triangle into the center of the room. She'd been completely suspended from it before, held safe in a rope body harness, wrists and ankles securely cuffed to the bars.

Today, however, Chase did not bind her. "I just want you to hold on. The bars give you something to grip. Lean forward and take hold. Ass out, but not too far. You can take the cane more easily if you're closer to a standing position. That way the muscles are relaxed." He stroked her ass as he said this, cupping the cheeks and then giving her a playful swat.

"Don't look so serious, sweetheart. This is for you, for us. This is our next step. I'm going to cane you and you're going to fly. Then I'm going to make love to you. Does that suit you?"

"Yes, Sir." Kate smiled. She did understand now, and embrace, her need for erotic pain. He'd introduced her to the flogger, the crop, his hand when she lay over his knee. Sometimes during the sessions he bound her in very tight, difficult positions, other times he had her maintain her own position, admonishing her to maintain it when she fell out of line after a particularly cruel stroke caught her skin.

She almost found the bondage easier, in that she wasn't required to exercise her own will. On the other hand, she appreciated Chase's sensitivity regarding the caning. Brighton had bound her, leaving her helpless to resist him. He'd ignored her cries and even her safeword. Chase, she knew, would never ignore her, focused as he always was on the slightest nuance of her reactions.

She gripped the bars and leaned slightly forward. Chase moved behind her, wrapping her body in his arms. "My beautiful sub girl," he said. "Are you ready to suffer for me?"

Kate shivered in his arms, but nodded. "Yes, Sir."

He retrieved the cane, a larger, thicker cane than the one Master John had used. "A beginner's cane," he had explained to Kate. "The thinner canes are whippier and can cut the skin. You'll see this one is easier to take."

He started very lightly, a simple tapping against her flesh, keeping the strokes confined to the fleshy padding of her bottom. She relaxed, leaning her head against one of the bars. She could do this.

"A little harder now," he warned. She practiced her breathing, slowly in and out, as the strokes began to sting. They were still fast and fairly light, moving steadily with a thwacking sound.

After several minutes of this, Kate began to feel the warm, buttery feeling easing its way through her body. The sting was real, but it was overlain with a sexual pleasure, an aching desire, that made it easier to bear.

As if he could feel what she was feeling, Chase murmured, "That's right. Good, Kate. Ease into it. It's time now."

She didn't have time to tense at this last remark before the first real stroke caught her smartly across both cheeks. "Ah!" she cried as a line of fire made itself felt. He struck her again, just below the first spot and she cried out again.

"Good. Keep your position. Very good, sub girl." Chase's voice had taken on the low purr, laced with steel, that he used when concentrating during a session. The strokes had hurt, but Kate found herself thrusting back, her skin tingling for another stroke, and another.

Unlike the scene at the BDSM party, here was no panic, no loss of control, no being obliterated by someone else's careless cruelty. Chase was making love to her, as he always did in their D/s play. The cane had become an extension of himself.

Kate opened herself to his loving, fiery attention, feeling her skin burn, along with her pussy, which throbbed. "Ten on each side," he informed her. "Don't worry about counting. Just go with it. Become one with it, with me. We'll fly together, my love."

She fell into a rhythm of pleasure and pain, surging and washing over her with each whoosh and strike of the rod against tortured flesh. Her mind went blank. She could feel music in her veins. There was no longing or hope, or past or future. There was only this moment, this time, now. Her skin turned to fire and she was lost in the brightness. She sailed, she soared, she floated and fell back into his arms...

~*~

Chase cradled Kate in his arms, his hand on her cheek. He'd caught her as she fell, dropping the cane in a clatter, worried for a moment he'd taken her too far. Then he saw the bliss of angels in her face, and felt the slow, steady beat of her heart against him, and was reassured.

He lifted her into his arms and carried her to the bedroom. He would have been content to let her rest, to let her float in that ephemeral nirvana for as long as she could. But she reached out for him. "I want you," she murmured. "Inside me. Please."

Who could resist such a sweet, wanton plea? Mindful of her welted ass, Chase entered her carefully. He'd been thrilled and humbled by her shaving her pussy for him. He'd never asked her to do that, and he found her lovely either way, but the gesture had moved him.

He held her, moving slowly, savoring her sweet sighs and the patter of her heart against his chest. He kissed her hair, keeping one hand on her cheek as he moved inside her. He could feel her returning from the secret, bright place the cane had taken her to, and felt a pang of regret, but this was soon lost in the pleasure of her body beneath his.

She surged beneath him, undulating in a way that sent ripples of pleasure through him. His balls tightened and he knew he was going to come too fast if she kept it up. He knew she needed more time to reach the pinnacle of pleasure and he wanted to give that to her. He shifted, trying to diffuse the hot, velvet grip of her cunt around him. But she was relentless, locking her strong legs around him and pulling him deep inside as she continued to swivel and glide beneath him.

"Kate," he managed. "Slow down, I'm going to..."

"I want you to," she whispered back fiercely. "You, just for you. This is for you, my love. Come for me. Come *to* me. Come to me, Chase. I belong to you."

He gave in, letting the climax overtake him as he clung to her, nearly faint with pleasure. When he was done, Kate still beneath him, he tried to move, to give her the chance to come, but she stopped him. "Lie still, my love. Rest." She stroked his back and he did as she asked, too spent to assert his will.

He appreciated now, perhaps better than he ever had, that D/s was a circle, the submission offered freely, taken with care and passion, returned with fire and love. It wasn't the trappings—the rope, the cane, the gear—that made D/s come alive. It wasn't even the D/s play itself—the erotic torture, the bondage, the claiming of one person by the other. He understood this now in a way he never had with any other woman, or even in his own mind. It was the *love* that made it all come alive, that brought it all full circle. *That* was the heart of submission.

Also Available at Romance Unbound Publishing

(http://romanceunbound.com)

The Solitary Knights of Pelham Bay

Texas Surrender

Cast a Lover's Spell

Sarah's Awakening

Wicked Hearts

Submission Times Two

Confessions of a Submissive

A Princely Gift

Accidental Slave

Slave Girl

Lara's Submission

Slave Jade

Obsession

Golden Angel: Unwilling Sex Slave

The Toy

Frog

Connect with Claire
Website: http://clairethompson.net
Indie Publishing Site: http://romanceunbound.com
Yahoo Chat Group:
http://groups.yahoo.com/group/clairethompson
Claire' Blog:
http://clairethompsonauthor.blogspot.com
Twitter: http://twitter.com/CThompsonAuthor
Facebook:
http://facebook.com/s.php?init=q&q=clairethompsona
uthor&ref=ts

Made in the USA
San Bernardino, CA
23 June 2016